The
Brahan
Seer

The Brahan Seer

The Story of Scotland's Nostradamus

A novel by
Douglas Thompson

With an introduction by
Margaret Elphinstone

acair

First published in 2014 by Acair Ltd.,
An Tosgan, Seaforth Road,
Stornoway, Isle of Lewis HS1 2SD

info@acairbooks.com
www.acairbooks.com

Book design by Graham Starmore, Windfall Press
Cover artwork by Jade Starmore

A CIP catalogue record for this title is available from
the British Library.

Printed and bound by Hussar Books, Poland.

Tha Acair a' faighinn taic bho Bhòrd na Gàidhlig.

ISBN   978-0-86152-562-1

Publisher's Note

Versions of parts of chapters 8, 11 and 12 appeared as the short story entitled *Finding Coinneach Odhar* awarded second prize in the Neil Gunn Writing Competition 2007, and published thereafter on the *Am Baile* website.

A version of chapter 3 appeared in *Random Acts of Writing* magazine Issue 11, October 2008, under the title *Freasdal: Raising Coinneach Odhar*.

A version of Chapters 1 and 2 appeared in *Visionary Tongue* magazine Issue 27, 2011, under the title *Providence*.

Foreword

Some four centuries ago Coinneach Odhar - better known today as the Brahan Seer - was tormented by strange, troubling visions far beyond the scope of ordinary men. Contemporary Scots are living in the future he foretold. I speak no Gaelic, and have seldom seen Coinneach's prophecies written down, but, like many others, I already knew about the nine bridges over the Ness, the metal geese in flight, the four fair sons of the last Mackenzie of Seaforth, the waters rising to the Eagle Stone, the invasion of Loch Eriboll... I also knew what happened to Coinneach Odhar. Someone must have told me these stories: I can't remember who or when. But the fact that they were already in my mind is proof that Gaelic oral tradition is alive and well. It affirms that languages that lie alongside each other can be conduits rather than barriers. For Coinneach too, translation is a crucial issue, as he struggles to find words for insights not yet thought of. The languages, traditions and narratives of our collective past are there to be shared and passed on, first, second or third hand, for as many generations as Coinneach himself could see. And in *The Brahan Seer*, even Coinneach sees no final ending.

Douglas Thompson's re-vision of Coinneach's story gives a new twist to this still-evolving narrative. Its written form and its emphasis on inner experience are modern: it is, after all, a novel. As such, it is utterly convincing: this is what it was like to be Coinneach himself. This is how he experienced the visions that shaped his life. This is what he felt about the cruel burden of prophecy that he carried, made worse by the knowledge that even though he could see so much, he could change nothing. We may not all be prophets, but in a more muted way Coinneach's dilemma is recognisable to us all.

The narrative strands - Coinneach's life story and the stories of past, present and future he is impelled to tell - come together through the land they share. Time collapses, but land endures. The stories written into the land are revealed to Coinneach, wherever he goes in his journeyings across the Highlands and islands of Scotland, from his birth in Lewis through all his wanderings to his death in the Black Isle. Coinneach, a deeply compassionate man and a sincere Christian, accepts with fortitude his experience of an eternal present, sometimes benign but often cruel. For him there is no doctrine involved, no argument over free will or predestination, heaven or hell, or any other preoccupation of church or state. It is simply *Freasdal* - providence. Coinneach's innocence, just as much as his inexplicable power, makes his own end inevitable.

Words give meaning to the land, and the land brings out the words. The connection between the two is alive for Coinneach's author just as it is for Coinneach himself. In *The Brahan Seer* it manifests in lyrical prose often drifting into poetry. Words fly away into the landscape, describing a stark, dangerous, frightening and yet uncannily beautiful world. Coinneach, whose mission is to voice the destiny of his people, has his origins in a half-bestial, half-supernatural Other which is rooted in the land. Poetry and prophecy enter his soul even as he is begotten in violence and fear. He is a normal, cheerful child, whose happiness is threatened by his perilous powers of perception. He grows into a man among men, except for his preternatural awareness of inner worlds and other times. Once again, the extraordinary is only the ordinary in another form. Thompson's Coinneach Odhar is alien, powerful and inexplicable, and yet he never ceases to be one of us.

Whether the Brahan Seer existed or not is neither here nor there. Perhaps there was a real Coinneach Odhar Mackenzie. Perhaps, as *The Brahan Seer* suggests, there were two Seers, whose lives spanned a century. Perhaps there were many such seers, and legend has combined them into one. The prophecies of the Brahan seer could be merely a post-industrial fiction; maybe the Brahan Seer exists in our imaginations simply because we need him. Prophecy, or second sight, is rooted in the Seer's country, and those who belong there have to engage with it in one way or another. One thing is certain: stories are told and re-told because they speak to the condition of their times. *The Brahan Seer* speaks to our condition, irrespective of past or future, because the story of Coinneach Odhar is a story about us.

Margaret Elphinstone

Margaret Elphinstone is a novelist and
Emeritus Professor at the University of Strathclyde

Part One

Chapter One

An arrowhead lodges itself into the trunk of a birch tree, and an old man runs past, breathless, escaping into the dense forest on the shores of Loch Ness. He moves ever upward, clambering on the steep mossy banks in the half-light beneath the forest canopy. Behind him, he sees the glimpses of colour of the soldiers' livery, as they fan out, shouting to each other, moving in and out of view behind the shifting fingers of bark. He is dressed in a curious white robe, his skin is unusually dark and lined, his features almost eastern, even Romany.

He runs at surprising speed, fit and lean, then, looking upwards then behind him again, rapidly ascends a pine tree, shuffling aloft into the canopy of needles. Time passes. Sunlight swims in his eyes. At times he hears only his own breath, then the breathing and sighing of the forest itself. He regards it as an ally, a guardian spirit whose secret the soldiers cannot understand. He mutters an ancient prayer under his breath, communes with the elves to protect him.

Suddenly he wakes up to see that a soldier is below him, taking a rest, drinking from his canteen. A pine cone dislodges itself from beneath the old man's feet and falls; every inch a mile in its long silent plummet. He sees that the spirit of the forest has betrayed him, that he has been abandoned by horned Cernunnos to the lust of slavering Esus, the ever-dying one. So be it. The pine cone reaches the earth and crunches loudly, the soldier looks up into the tree, and the old man falls on him, drawing a silver sickle from his robes. Only the very start of a cry leaves his mouth before the old man's fingers close it, while his other hand cuts his throat expertly. He feels the soldier's strength ebb away, and he crouches there in silence over the body, slowing his breath, listening for any of his comrades who may be coming, as a pool of warm blood spreads over the pine needles.

~

The old man's sickle slices through the stocks of mushrooms, lifting them reverently to his nose, placing them on a wooden pan that he unhooks from his belt. He plucks mistletoe from a bush that is clinging around the base of an oak tree, crushing the leaves with a pestle. He finds poppies further on, in another clearing, from which he collects the seeds, then takes whole branches of yew and binds them into a load for his back.

He pushes his head out from a thicket at the forest's edge, from where he can see a distant homestead, see sheep and lambs grazing in the fields. He slips along the perimeter of the forest for half a mile then edges out on hands and knees. A lamb turns to look at him curiously and he thrusts a handful of crushed herbs under its nostrils until its eyes close.

~

The old man lifts his head towards the sun, and having reached the edge of a great wilderness finally emerges from the forest into the light. With the yew branches and herbs and a lamb trussed up on his back, he begins a long climb up a vast slope of grass and moorland, muttering to himself in some ancient tongue.

The shadows of clouds play slowly across the slope on which he walks, like a tiny ant progressing methodically, as the hours pass on a long midsummer day.

~

At the hill's summit, a flat elliptical plane is adorned with a stone circle, and at its centre, a menhir made of three balanced stones, a rough-hewn altar. He makes his way to its centre, then sits cross-legged, closes his eyes and begins an incantation.

He takes wood and begins a fire, mixes sacred paint to apply to his face and arms in patterns of curving, interlacing knotwork, all the while singing in the same ancient language. He nods his head back and forward, closing his eyes, offering prayers to Taranis, God of thunder.

He boils the mushrooms and poppy seeds, and drinks them greedily. His pupils begin to dilate, his singing growing louder.

~

He raises his sickle to the sky, and screams wildly, eyes vanished into his forehead, then turns around and plunges the blade into the lamb and cuts it once laterally, once vertically, and pulls its limbs in different directions.

He lifts his hand to his face and smears his lips and forehead with blood, chanting rhythmically, reaching into the sheep's innards.

He eats the heart raw, and then unwinds the intestines in different directions, reaching down from the altar and stretching out towards specific stones in the circle.

He turns the empty stomach towards the rising moon, as evening falls, and takes more of the fermented mushrooms, burning yew leaves and bark on the fire and inhaling their aroma until his whole mind is a vast arena where the Gods dance and make war. He feels he is a conduit, a sacred well through which the spirit-world can re-emerge into the everyday.

The Gods are ruthless, they might destroy him eventually, wound him or others, or make all manner of havoc in this world. But this is the price they exact for the knowledge they impart, the clues they leave in the ashes after their departure, fragments of past and future, spells and portents. It is dangerous to listen in like this, on the games of the Divine Ones, but more dangerous still to oppose them, to deny them entry into our bodies. They often long for flesh and blood.

He dreams the high sky passes, clouds falling like flags unfurled, the armies of men clashing endlessly, their armour as the shells of insects, crushed into the brown earth. He sees the hidden roots, the white tree that grows upside down beneath the world's heart, where all lives and deaths join together. Shining metal birds fly overhead, fingers of glass rise on the horizon like supplicating hands. His heartbeat races like a drum beneath the deepest ocean until his veins are the veins on the leaf of the hidden tree. He flows in the green blood, circulates from root to sap, becomes hunched, foetus-like in the new buds, gnawing on his own bones, blowing ash into the eye of life.

~

Chapter Two

At low tide, the pale bright sands stretch to the horizon. With the sun high in the sky, and the sea a distant mirage in flickering heat, this could be a desert, a vast natural arena. The villagers are gathered around a wedding ceremony, having been led down onto the beach by their minister, climbing over his stone dyke from the glebe, to walk barefoot across the machair, their feet sinking in the dunes. Voices, laughter, scatter into musical fragments, blown by the summer wind. The Bible is held high, sand shaken from robes, the reading commences.

As the minister's voice rings out across the sand, the savage mountains behind to the south seem to rise up now like a diagram of gravity and fatality. Their mottled black hues, studded with glimmers of quartz, are like the binding of a Bible yet more ancient, untranslatable, unopened. The bride's long blonde hair is adorned with rare flowers gathered from the bleak peat moors that reach inland for interminable distances. The groom's plaid of finest lambswool, dyed in modest hues of brown and green, is still rough and itchy on his skin, woven for this day. Both their heads are bowed in solemn deference to these words that sanctify their union, Gaelic vowels and syllables taking flight into the sun, diadems of silver light sparkling, the distant sea encroaching, grains of sand accumulating on their collars, in their hair.

~

Later, the sands seem to glow luminous white in the twilight, as the dancing continues and music spins and weaves on the beach, a bonfire lit, the faces animated by red flames.

The bride and groom hurry laughing past the whitewashed cottages of the village, and climb the pasture towards their own house, built for them by the groom's brothers. Cows turn their curious eyes towards them in the half-light, unaccustomed to their new owners, horns strangely prominent in the moonlight.

Inside, the ocean seems almost louder. It enters the windows and makes the walls and the house its own, like a cave of the sea. Lying together on the straw mattress, the waves seem to sift and caress the lovers' minds, a sound they have each heard since birth. Like the tethered boats on the bay as the tide rises, they kiss and nudge together in sympathy with the ancient motion of the earth and moon.

~

In the early morning, the blonde bride, now wife to Coinneach mac Choinnich, Kenneth son of Kenneth, leaves the cottage to let the sheep into higher pasture. She is inexperienced, and a ewe bolts past her and escapes the wooden gate by the stone dyke, and gallops upwards towards the scree slopes, braying defiantly. Uncertain, she hovers then returns to the door of the cottage. Seeing her husband is still sleeping, she puts on a shawl and sets off to retrieve the sheep.

The weather is less certain than the day before, a few clouds lick the slopes of the mountain she is climbing. Terrace after terrace of sheep tracks, worn over centuries, reach up into the mist, their narrow widths somehow distorting any sense of scale. The sheep dislodges a stone above her, and she clings close to the slope to let it bounce safely past.

At length the sheep leads her past the base of a cliff and through a fissure into a hidden valley; a shady corrie where a cool black lochan sits still as a mirror, beyond which another smooth slope strewn with black boulders leads upwards to a high plain.

She sees the sun is rising higher in the sky, the shadows shortening, thinks she still has ample time to return before her husband wakes. She walks, as in a dream, past the black lochan towards the haunting shape of the natural gateway to the plain above. Odd-shaped boulders are scattered on every side, the lochan's water is murky brown from the exposed peat and heather roots around its eroded banks. The sheep now frolics ahead with strange confidence, as if at home in this realm, looking back mockingly.

On the high plain, she finds a view of immense empty boglands, falling away into the distance, dotted with silver and blue fragments of sky: countless pools and sinks. She is so entranced for a moment by the scale of this vista, that she forgets the ewe, until she hears a sudden bleating cry somewhere behind her, followed by a series of dull blows.

She follows the sound, moving off to her right until a sunken hollow is revealed, sudden outcrops of rock leading down to a lowered plain where a white figure is bowed over the sheep. For a second she doesn't take in the whole scene. A strange gantry of gnarled driftwood branches spans the gulley behind him: with animal skins and bones hanging in odd ritualistic postures. Bleached skulls are arranged in piles around an ash circle where Pictish symbols have been inscribed and obsessively overlaid. Returning her eyes to the centre of the scene, she sees the old man's hands moving inside the sheep's stomach, its legs still kicking. Involuntarily she cries out in revulsion. His face turns up instantly, a terrible face, eyes black and ruthlessly alert, skin brown and snakelike.

It happens too fast, as if he knows she was there, wanted her to see and be transfixed before he flicked his eyes up. The red tongue moves out, the eyes expand baring their whites, and dropping the sheep, he plunges forward and upwards with enormous speed, his hands and forearms steeped in blood like long red gloves.

She screams and runs, mouth and heart open to the sky, the sun suddenly mute behind twisting grey veils of cloud and mist. She feels her heart pound, blood in her ears, the force of her footfalls reverberating through her body, before the green moor lurches up to meet her, tasting her own teeth, her nose pressing into moss and stones.

Something blunt hits her head, and a rock lands on the ground next to her, and she only seems to be able to look at this rock for the next minute, as she splits into two: one living, one watching. His hands are on her, lifting up her dress. A cold breeze runs up her stomach, then she feels his strange breath on her hair, her ears, odour of garlic and stale flesh. A stone pressing against her, a message pressed into her head: *wake up, save yourself while you can, now*. The two people writhing, pinned, become one again, living and watching: his hand moves over her thigh, while her hand hidden moves down to take a knife from her belt. He tenses, and lets out a short screeching like an eagle with its talons on a rabbit, as an arrow goes through its breast. She twists her legs around until she lifts his body and sees his face, eyes rolling, her knife in his neck up to the hilt. She brings her knees up, and kicks him backwards, arching through the air onto a rock. She follows after him, and pulls the knife out with both hands, rolls on the grass, then dives back onto him, screaming like a wild animal, plunging the knife into his chest repeatedly, unnecessarily. He is a just a carcass now, a grey felled beast, head leant back, eyes open towards the moor, the pools of reflected sky, diminishing into the distance. Only her breath now, and the wind.

Her eyes alight for a second on the strange carved circular stones on a leather thong around his waist, the dark blue twisting tattoos on his arms, designs she recognises from standing stones.

She spits on him, then begins sobbing, wailing like a wounded animal, a body without thought, staggering in blood and rags back towards the black lochan. She stumbles into it, crying out, washing her skin and hair, her fingers thrust inside herself, blood diffusing in twisting clouds underwater, moving off into darkness.

~

Chapter Three

Coinneach Mackenzie, 3 years old, sits by the window and plays with green bottles he has found on the beach. Singing to himself, he looks through the glass at the distorted view to the sea outside, then turns to look out at his mother washing sheets in a tub, her figure dwarfed by the dark room swollen to vast proportions. He drums his bare feet on the rough-hewn edges of the stone flags, laughs at the stray lamb that runs in and out of the open doorway.

He talks to his imaginary friends, who tell him stories of strange people who have lived and died in other houses, who whisper to him, sometimes asking him to do things. *Tell her about Hector's boat*, they say today, *the blue shirt in Mangersta Bay.*

Mamaidh... the green spirit wants me to tell you something...

His mother looks up; *-Coinneach, go and play outside in the light, I have no time for your daft games today.*

It's about Uncle Hector... he says, tentatively, and notices her pausing a little. She moves to continue working, but the voices say: *more, more, the boat and the shirt, Coinneach...*

Waterhorse says Hector wore a blue shirt and the boat was called Bethany...

Mamaidh puts one hand to her throat, and another against the wall to steady herself, staring at the floor, the bedsheet in her hands falling away.

What's wrong Mamaidh? –he says, going over, green bottle in his hand, *-yellow bird says Hector sleeps at Mangersta, between two rocks the shape of loaves, studded with black barnacles...*

His mother suddenly falls on him, and knocks the bottle away, smashing it into fragments, splitting light from the window into wheeling blades. Her face is sweating up close to his, blonde hair fallen over her eyes, her expression wild with fear or madness. She makes a weird snivelling noise as she pins him against the wall, knocking the wind out of him, hurting his chest. *Mamaidh…* he tries to say, tears beginning to sob from his body, as she rasps at him:

Who told you to say these things? Tell me!? How do you know these things about Hector? You're frightening me Coinneach… why!? Her arms loosen and she slumps to the floor, eyes empty, as Coinneach runs out the door wailing, the lamb running after him.

~

On Mangersta beach, a group of fishermen walk across the sand in drizzling rain, in strange brown autumnal light, broad oilskin hats and knee-high boots, oil lamps and ropes in their hands. Black clouds spew inwards to the dim halo of the muted sun. Slops of sky-mirror wipe out their footprints behind them like slow brush strokes from right to left.

At the twin rock outcrops one man hangs back, hands nervously brushing over the texture of tiny black mussel shells which encase the whole rock like a skin. The older man ahead kneels to examine a body half-buried in the sand. Coinneach's father, eyes dark with foreboding, lifts the oil-lamp higher. A fragment of blue shirt twists in the wind between a broken creel and a clump of seaweed. Curved shards of painted boat-planks emerge from the sand, strewn wooden bones.

As the wind whistles, a weather-worn hand, cuff of thick-woven wool; moves over the plank's surface, removing sand to reveal white and gold faded stencilling: *B-E-T-H-A-N-Y*

~

Coinneach is woken in the middle of the night to see his father and one of the Church Elders looking in at his cot, candle held aloft.

Coinneach… his father says softly, *how did you learn of what you told your mother about Uncle Hector? Who told you? Did you overhear some adults talking about him?*

No, Coinneach says sleepily, sweetly. *The spirits told me. Greenheart and Waterhorse I think, they seemed to know most about it…*

His father looks at the Church Elder and then back at Coinneach, now caressing his hair, -*Conn, do you understand that Hector is drowned? Your mother's brother, Coinneach?*

Not dead… sleeping… mumbles Coinneach cheerily. The wind blows through the rafters, creaking like a boat.

The Elder takes the candle and leans in closer: *Coinneach, can you tell us who Greenheart is, and where you think Hector is now?*

Greenheart is Greenspirit, lives in grass blades and leaves, Guardian of animals…

And Hector?

Waterhorse embraced him to stop him being lonely and brought him home, now he lives with Greenheart forever, happier now…

Coinneach nods off to sleep again, as the two adults are left staring into space above his head, a single tear now forming in his father's eye.

~

A little older now, Coinneach runs behind his father, as they gather the cattle together on the high moor. Their dog darts back and forward, running up and down, tongue hanging out. Coinneach keeps turning, looking back to where the sea glitters on the horizon.

As his father rests on the ground, bonnet pulled down over his head, the dog watches off to one side, its yellow eyes flicking between him and the cows. Coinneach's little shadow falls over him: *Athair? Where does the sun go?*

Down below the horizon for the night, Conn, like you going to your bed.

But why does it rise and fall in different places?

It's the seasons, son, autumn and winter and spring, the sun goes off to the south them times of year, like geese flying south for the winter.

Are people like the sun, Athair? Do they come back?

His father breathes out and thinks for a while, then tilts his bonnet up, squints at his boy, sunlight in his eyes: *One day son, yes. When The Lord calls on them… he'll go around waking them all up on the Day of Judgement. But the Minister tells it much better than me… He says it will be quite a sight to see.*

Will I see it?

That you will, Conn, and you'll hold your head high that day, knowing you have served the Lord well.

While his father sleeps, Coinneach climbs the slope behind him, hoping to see more of where the sun goes to hide, where Jesus keeps the dead people. He climbs higher than he plans, the view, the cool air exhilarating him, until he can see a whole spread of the horizon, but disappointed: finds no more of the sun's bed is on show.

In the gulley behind him he finds bones and ashes and sticks. He plays with a few of them, and a weird stone rolls away past his feet. Something about it catches his eye. He runs after it, just capturing it before it rolls off towards the cliffs, and lifts it up to examine.

Blowing the dirt from it, he sees that its grey surface is incised with complex snakelike patterns, like some of the carvings he has seen in the churchyard. It is an almost perfect disk with a hole in the middle. He smiles and puts it away into his shirt pocket, and begins scrambling back down towards his father, hearing his voice calling to him.

~

Coinneach's little brother opens his eyes and mouth and wails in wordless indignation. His mother lifts him out of the cot and pats his back and bottom, rocking him back to sleep. She sits back down in an old wooden chair by the cottage door, white sand blowing over her feet. As the baby sleeps, her neighbour talks quietly to her:

He is very fair and blue-eyed like yourself, Issy, not at all like Coinneach... That boy's growing so dark and swarthy these days, he's like a proper little gypsy...

Coinneach's mother slows her motions, stops rocking the baby, her eyes suddenly completely vacant, staring down at the sand.

Issy? Issy? Her neighbour shakes her, *I was saying maybe it's all the long walks he's been taking with his father makes him so dark...? Issy...?*

~

Coinneach stands over the cradle, and smiles down at his little brother. Blonde Ruaraidh stares back and looks like he's about to cry. Coinneach produces his carved stone like a magic trick and rolls it in his fingers and Ruaraidh starts laughing, amused by the shadow it throws, the beam of sunlight that falls through it.

Suddenly his mother crosses the threshold and looks at them. Coinneach's fingers stop moving, the stone hovers. He continues to move forward for a second then flicks his eyes up to meet hers. In a flash, she sees not Coinneach's eyes but the crazed eye of the devil on the moor, the carved stones around his belt.

She leaps on him: *Coinneach, give me that stone...*

No! He wails, *it's mine... it's my secret!*

She screams and shoves him against the wall, the baby starting to cry. *Where did you get this stone, Coinneach? You MUST tell me, it's very, very important, you must give it to me...*

No! He wails and runs away pursued by her, her hands flailing and chastising him.

With the skill of a conjurer, a tiny clod of turf has been squeezed back into place behind him, in a space between two of the rocks in the wall, concealing the magic stone, as he misdirects his pursuer.

~

As his mother sits alone in the kirk, praying and whispering at a bench near the front, the figure of Coinneach appears at the door, bright wind-blown machair behind him.

Buzzards ate him... he mumbles.

What did you say? She whispers, eyes staring straight ahead, then turning around, wiping her eyes to confront him, trying to stay calm. *What did you just say there, Coinneach?*

He smiles sleepily. *Yellow Bird says the buzzards ate him up, the Bad Fox, says Mamaidh's not to be frightened now...*

Who is the Bad Fox, Coinneach?

Was... he corrects, *WAS. He's just bones now, can't hurt no one.*

Who, Coinneach? Who was he? She runs her hand over her neck, shivering.

Coinneach looks up into the roof, then closes his eyes for a second, then opens them, whispering excitedly: *Demon,*

*from the Moon Time, hurt Mamaidh, gave Coinneach eyes of
an eagle.*

A crow suddenly crashes into the high window behind
them: they both scream, its black shape sliding down the
gothic tracery, leaving a smear of blood. Coinneach starts
to giggle, and his mother spins around and slaps him, then
grabs his hand fiercely and marches him out, slamming the
thick wooden door behind them.

~

It is one of Coinneach's first days away on his own. He has
worked a hard four hours lifting peats on the high moor on
the slopes of *Forsnaval*, and now he throws himself down
on the ground to have his lunch. His father is somewhere
almost in sight on the other side of the valley, helping a
friend harvest barley. Autumn is on the way, the sky has a
harsher light, the clouds patterned like hoarfrost.

He unwraps his knapsack, and takes a few bites of his
mother's bannock, thinking the jam is a little on the sharp
side today, maybe the brambles aren't in season yet.

Remembering his stone, he takes it from his tunic pocket
with a feeling of guilty joy. His superstitious mother must
think it is stolen from a church vestry or something. She
has a horror of pagan relics, but has never managed to steal
it from him. He looks at it, and runs his fingers over its
fine knotwork decoration, enjoying its texture, proud of his
lucky talisman.

His head nods forward, he shivers, he feels a sharp pain
in his stomach. He looks back at the stone, and finds his
eyesight is going blurred. He looks off to the moor, then
up at the sky, another stab in his stomach: his vision swims
and he clutches the stone then throws his fist open, crying
out. The centre of the ring itself seems on fire, as if it is the

centre of his stomach, the source of all his pain. Like a navel through which he can unmake his own birth, go backwards or forwards, inside out. The pain stabs again and he lurches forward into the fire, the mirror; the scene that plays there at its centre:

He sees his mother crossing the village late at night, a deep blue twilight under a sickle moon, a shawl pulled up over her head, as she walks along the side of the road towards Aird Uig, to consult old Aghi of the potions. Everyone knows her house by its half-collapsed thatch, the old blackened wind-torn tree that grows through its gable. Aghi leads her inside and shows her some mice. She takes out a black bottle and pours a little of the dark green liquid onto some cheese and puts it under the mouse's nose. It eats greedily, but before it has finished begins to move its legs erratically, to spit and hiss. It writhes in agony, blood spilling from its mouth and anus, and then lies dead. Old Aghi cackles and sells her the bottle for a few coins, wishing her luck with the rats. He sees his mother rising early next day and dropping spots of the poison onto his bannock, onto the bramble jam…

The stone spins out of his hand as he falls onto his side, screaming, twisting, blood foaming from his nostrils, vomit burning his throat. The world goes grey then silent, then very far away.

~

He regains consciousness in his bed as his father and a physician from Stornoway lean over him. His vision swims weakly, one whole side of his face is grotesquely swollen up, his right eye caked in dried blood. He sweats and shakes as the cool hands stroke his forehead.

The boy may be disfigured for life, Mackenzie, but he will live and see, with one eye at least. He is lucky to be alive.

Coinneach tries to speak, but finds his lips and tongue too distorted to form the words. He can hear his mother's deranged wailing and weeping in the next room. He reaches out and draws with his finger in the dust on the floor. The physician raises the oil lamp to see the symbol he is drawing: a bottle with a skull-and-bones on it. *We know, Coinneach, we know it was poison... it's all right...* his father says softly.

Who, Coinneach, who? asks the doctor.

Coinneach starts to move his finger again, then stops and looks at his father. He gestures for him to lean down, and then whispers in his ear, forcing his lips into shape until they spit.

They clasp hands, and look again into each other's eyes again for a long time.

~

Chapter Four

Fairburn Castle estate, Inverness-shire, spring of 1652.

Coinneach's one good eye is out of focus, he is staring off into space dreaming, remembering, as somebody is talking to him:

Mackenzie! Coinneach Mackenzie! I asked you a question, man. How came you by your disfigurement, and are you fit?

The man seated at the wooden trestle in the cobbled yard is head groundsman and site foreman, flanked by a clerk and provisioner. In front of him Coinneach Mackenzie stands at the head of a line of itinerant farm hands reporting for work at the start of a new season.

It was the scarlet fever sir, he lies, *it claimed my sight in one eye, and it makes my smile a little crooked on this side, but other than that I am as fit as an ox.*

And have you worked on other farms, can you lift a hundredweight sack of wood or neeps if a foreman takes a notion to hurl one on your back?

Yes sir, I have lifted worse.

And did the fever claim any others in your household?

My mother, sir, God rest her soul.

Go on then, sign your name here, or make your mark or whatever. Your pay will be four shillings a week, as long as the work lasts, plus food and lodgings. Take a blanket from our Màiri, then you'll be shown a byre you can sleep in for the first month, after that we might find you a place in one of the cottages up the road.

Coinneach moves on and finds himself facing Màiri Chisholm. Their eyes meet and she smiles modestly at him, averting her gaze quickly. *Good day to you miss,* he says, then adds, thinking: *have we met in the past?*

She shakes her head silently, dismissively, handing him a folded blanket. He turns away, running his hand through his thick unruly hair, then hesitates and turns back, raising a finger inquisitively: *then have we met in the future?*

Her eyes darken and cloud with suspicion, and he furrows his brow also, peering into her face. *Yes... that will be what it is then*, he says brightly.

Oh, be off with you, she whispers. He strolls off and she shakes her head looking after him in bemusement.

~

Walking through the woods from the stables, Coinneach sees two men up ahead, engaged in a heated argument next to an old millpond. As he approaches, he slows down and moves more quietly and carefully, stopping to observe them for a second from the shadows. He watches their gestures closely, as their voices rise higher, and they begin to push each others' chests.

Coinneach suddenly strides out from the shadows and arrives at the back of one of the men just as he is reaching an arm around to a pocket at his back. He catches the arm, and pulls it out and around, revealing that it is now holding a dagger, as its owner exclaims: *What, who are you? Thieving gypsy bastard, let go!*

What's this? The other man now exclaims, *you would stab me, Davie?*

Coinneach prises the dagger out of the man's hand, tosses it into the millpond, punches him in the face, knocking him to the ground, then shakes the hand of the man left standing, who amazed, says: *Andrew Grant, sir, pleased to make your acquaintance... oops.*

The man lying on the ground rises and they both turn

simultaneously and swing their fists and hit home, left and right-handed, a cheek each, and the fellow returns to the ground again, …. *and that was the unfortunate face of Davie Morrison!*

They continue shaking hands now, laughing.

Coinneach, or Kenneth, Mackenzie, sir.

I should tell you I usually fight my own battles, Coinneach.

Yes, but that was about to be a rather uneven battle my friend, and very possibly your last, since I would say you have no blade of your own about you.

They walk on together, leaving Davie behind to pick himself up gradually, a few friends arriving on the scene to help him.

But… Andrew thinks out loud, *how did you know he had a knife he was about to draw? I've never known him to do that before now, though we have often argued.*

Intuition, I suppose.

Women's intuition?

Coinneach turns to meet him, knitting his brow for a second and straightening his jaw, as if to fight, then seeing Andrew's smirk, laughs out loud: *Lewis Gaelic intuition !*

Ah yes, Andrew smiles, *of course, second-sight and all that business, that's quite an accent you have there, where do you hail from precisely? Skye? Assynt?*

Further still, Leodhas, Lewis, the Long Island as we call it.

And what brings you here, bold son of Kenneth?

The work. A man must eat. And curiosity I suppose. It is interesting to see buildings more than a storey high, "the devil's work" to a Lewisman of course (he parodies his own accent with the last phrase), *like that one…* He points towards what rises up on the hill ahead of them now: Fairburn Castle, a narrow six-storey tower house. *My father was a fisherman, but I didn't inherit his taste for it, my legs have always felt steadier on dry land, and my stomach more at peace.*

Well you have a stomach for a fight, Coinneach.

No, I do not, I avoid violence wherever I have a choice, since it is generally a costly matter among men, he shakes his head, slowing down for a second. *Your friend had decided to stab you; I can assure you his intention was not to spar but to strike you down outright. You should take care that he does not get an opportunity like that again.*

It's all right Coinneach, Andrew says, his face serious again, *I believe you… absolutely, I believe you.*

~

Out in the fields, Coinneach and Andrew and the other men are constructing a dry dyke. As the foreman supervises them, a human chain is ferrying the stones from a ruin in the woods. To save time, the supervisor has encouraged them to stand as far apart as possible, tossing the stones.

Still fuming, Davie Morrison sees to it that he swaps places with a friend so that he can stand next in line to Coinneach. The stones soon begin getting thrown off target, or too hard or too soft, as a demonic grimace spreads over Davie's face. Coinneach knows that if he lets any stone drop then the line will come to an end and he will draw the foreman's wrath, even have his wages docked. Coinneach locks eyes with Davie, and the rocks get faster and harder, but Coinneach keeps catching them. Davie tries to surprise him, flinging one suddenly to the left and right but Coinneach seems to be able to anticipate every action.

Gradually the whole line begins to notice the incredible force of the stones Davie is throwing and the foreman walks towards them to investigate. Still moving faster, Davie hurls a stone just as the foreman draws level with them and everything stops dead. People gasp. Davie stares disbelievingly with open hands, as he sees the foreman writing on the ground having received a stone straight in his groin from close quarters.

Some men are holding back laughter now, as Coinneach smiles grimly back at Davie, eyebrows raised, while Andrew and others run to attend to the foreman, the farmer's eldest son even being summoned to the scene. *He made me do it, this gypsy bastard...* Davie stammers, *I swear it on my mother's life, he's a sorcerer or something, he made my hands go the wrong way.*

As two men are led away, the foreman to have a long lie down, Davie to be paid off and sent on his way, the whole line finally breaks into laughter, and starts work again.

~

Màiri pauses at the head of the next dyke, carrying a basket of bread for the mid-day break, smiling vaguely at the eccentric figure Coinneach cuts, making the men laugh, impersonating the Doric accent of Davie Morrison as he swings the stones, in ever more exaggerated tones until he sounds like a cockerel.

~

Grey clouds are gathering for a squall of rain, as the men rest from digging a ditch for a waterlogged patch of field near the road to Muir of Ord.

An old woman suddenly appears at the hedgerow, calling on Coinneach. He looks about, thinking she must be talking to somebody else, but as everyone starts looking at him, feels compelled to go over and talk to her.

Ahh Coinneach Odhar Fiosaiche, here you are then, welcome back... She has wild bulbous eyes that seem to look in opposite directions at once.

I've only been in this parish but a few weeks, madam, begging your pardon, but are you mistaking me for someone else?

Oh no no, she says, *I know you well enough Coinneach Odhar, your fame precedes you. I salute you, sir!*

What did you call me? Odhar?

Yes, yes... she cackles, and tries to run her hands over his face as he recoils instinctively, *it is your nickname, that dark skin of yours, it is what everyone will call you soon.*

Where do you think you have seen me before?

Why Coinneach Odhar, I saw you only last night in a dream, leading a crowd across a bridge as a great flood swept away the stones of the arches from under them, but those that listened to you just kept walking and made it across on thin air, like ghosts they all were, grey as mist, walking on air...

Who are you? he asks, his eyes narrowing.

Ahh, now you're asking eh? But the rain's on soon, Coinneach, I best be away before it drowns me, Mad Margaret they call me in these parts.

The rain starts to pelt heavily, in dark clots, as Coinneach runs to catch up with the other men moving to shelter in the woods. He looks back over his shoulder to see the old woman is gone, but a sudden rainbow is appearing, landing almost where she stood.

"Odhar" did she call you? Andrew asks, smiling quizzically.

Yes... Odhar... the other men say, nodding, noting his unusually dark complexion, *I'd say that suits you well.*

I'm sure my father spoke of someone of that name years ago, some local rogue or outlaw or something, does anyone else remember that? Andrew muses, shaking the rain out of his hair.

No, don't think so... everyone else looks blankly, shaking their heads, *but the name does have a ring to it.*

Hey, that was Mad Maggie, Coinneach, Andrew says as Coinneach stares down into space, deep in thought, *a crazy old witch from Beauly, how come she was so taken with you?*

I don't know, Coinneach says quietly, furrowing his brow, eyes still far away, *truly... it was the strangest thing.*

~

Chapter Five

As the men are bedding down for the night on the floor of the barn, Màiri comes by, blowing out each of the oil lamps in turn.

Och Màiri, will you not come and bed down with us and the cattle? Come on, Màiri? -various jocular voices call from the darkness, protected by anonymity.

Andrew and Coinneach have been sitting talking by the stable doors, as she draws near. *Toch toch, Màiri, take no heed of them, they are little better than cattle themselves,* Andrew laughs.

Yes, and timid cattle at that, since I have noticed they are not so brave in daylight or when my father is about. She replies, coming closer.

Nor so brave as our new farm hand Coinneach here, from the Western Islands, he may have saved my life last week.

We have met, Màiri smiles at Coinneach, *you are the jester who mixes up his past and future, eh? What was the problem with you and the hot-headed Davie Morrison?*

He called me a gypsy and questioned my parentage.

Andrew laughs aloud: *Now was that not just a manner of speaking?*

And are you? Màiri asks eagerly, her eyes widening, *a gypsy I mean? Can you read my palm?*

Coinneach snorts, eyes Andrew slyly, then takes her hand anyway, pretends to examine the lines on it.

Well… what do you see? She asks.

What do you want to know? He replies, giving her hand back.

My fortune, of course, my future…

Long or short term?

Well, she laughs, *let us try long term first.*

It is clear. You will have two fine sons by a man born in a boat at midsummer, seven grandchildren, and you will live into your eighties.

And short term?

Nothing out of the ordinary. You will have a stiff neck tomorrow, and spend the evening by a waterfall. The day after that you will have unexpected news from a forgotten relative.

She smiles, whispering: *You made all that up did you not? What about my life line? You cannot read palms at all, you rogue!*

Quite so, he laughs, *just as I am no gypsy, but it was a fair pleasure to hold your hand for a moment and watch your wonderment, was it not?*

She makes to cuff him about the ear and he ducks back under the rafters and she puts the light out and hurries away, the sound of her shoes on the cobbles fading out, a distant door creaking shut, a bolt driven home.

Lying down in the darkness, he hears Andrew say: *That was mischievous of you, Coinneach, trying to embarrass me like that, making use of what I told you about my being born in a boat.*

You did not tell me that, Andrew.

Truly? About it being midsummer on the shore of Loch Leven, when my mother went into labour and sheltered in the hulk of an old sailboat to give birth?

No Andrew. But thank you for telling me of it now.

You are an uncanny fellow, Coinneach... but I think you might be tricking us all.

Coinneach snores.

~

While taking his midday break, Coinneach sees Andrew running towards him across the fields. *Coinneach, come and*

*see this, the Laird of Fairburn is making an announcement...
there is to be new work undertaken on the Towerhouse, good
money to be earned.* Coinneach stands up to join him and
they make their way there together.

Reaching the castle grounds just as the crowd is dispersing,
Andrew pores over some vellum plans laid out on a field
trestle, but notices after a while that Coinneach seems
uninterested. Coinneach backs away to get a better view of
the tower, just under the shade of the neighbouring woods.

When Andrew catches up with him, he notices that
Coinneach has some kind of stone up at his eyes, which he
puts hurriedly away. *What are you doing now, surveying the
place?* Coinneach doesn't answer.

Andrew sighs: *well, what do you say, man? I think I'll sign
up for a stint of that. I'm no mason, but even the labouring
pay, just lugging stones, would please me well.*

It is going to collapse... Coinneach says quietly.

Andrew laughs, taking this for a joke at first, *What? The
entire tower?*

*No. Although in a few centuries it will be ruinous, and the
laird's family destitute, but that is by the bye. At this moment I
speak only of the new works planned. This new stair wing will
collapse before it reaches over two storeys in height. Several
men will be killed or maimed for the head mason's mistakes.
Trust me, Andrew. Don't sign up for this until August, by
which time the project will be overseen by men of wiser mind.*

Andrew stands up and looks down at him in confusion
and sceptical disgust, the shadows of leaves playing over his
face. *Coinneach, you talk a mighty armada of hogwash of an
occasion, when you have wind in your sails, do you know that?*

Coinneach smiles and shrugs his shoulders. *As you wish,
get crushed alive, get both your legs broken, or your hands torn
off, be my honoured guest.*

~

Sitting in the local tavern, Andrew and Coinneach and some of the other hired hands are laughing and recounting tales. One lad, flagon lifted, is finishing a story: *...so the inn keeper says to me an ma wife oan oor wedding day "ah huv nine ordinary rooms like, but ah could gie you the bridal..." to which ah quipped nah nah dinnae bother man, ah'll jist haud on tae her hair as usual!*

Laughter erupts again, then the drinks are downed, empty flagons thumped on the table, and chairs scraped backwards across the worn floorboards. *Och well, it's time to gang up the road, the moon's high up above the trees noo.*

Andrew gestures to Coinneach and they stay behind for another drink.

So Coinneach, you won't have a change of heart about the Fairburn work?

I told you what I see.

But Coinneach, that is old woman's talk, I spoke to the site foreman and he said the head mason has not even been chosen yet, so how can you be sure he will be inexperienced or that he will make some big mistake, or do you have some secret experience of your own in masonry or groundworks? I mean, this does not make any sense does it?

The future cannot be changed.

You truly believe you can see the future?

I know I can.

Andrew snorts. *Prove it then, come on,* he says, finishing his ale, *show me some of these magical powers of yours, a demonstration now, please...*

Coinneach looks at him for a long while, then turns up his collar as they stand up to leave, and says: *Very well then, on the way up the lane, just after we pass an old cartwheel abandoned by the road, and as you look up at the moon through a gap in the trees, we will suddenly be attacked.*

Andrew looks down at him, amazed, as leaving the tavern,

Coinneach stretches into a thicket and pulls out two thick sticks to defend themselves with. *You will receive a flesh wound here,* he indicates his left cheek, *-and I will receive a cut to the back of my left forearm and the palm of my right hand. Don't worry, nobody is going to die.*

Coinneach, now you are concerning me a little. If you truly believe this then why did you not insist that we travel this road together with the other lads, not just the two of us?

Yes, but it was you who kept us behind, remember?

I think you're making one of your uncanny jests, tricking me for your amusement, eh?

Well, let us just stay alert. That is all I will say further on the matter.

They walk on, growing more silent and afraid as the woods get closer and the leaves arch in overhead.

The walk passes without incident and as they reach the end of the woods, Andrew says: *Och, Coinneach, that was a fine way to pull a fellow's leg. And there was me keeping my eyes down so that I wouldn't be tempted to look up at the moon. I mean if there was somebody there we would have heard their footsteps keeping pace with us by now...*

Not over the sound of the wind in the trees, and not if they walked on the moss in the woods, and besides they would need to hear us speak before they could be sure of our identities, something you have just provided them with...

Andrew laughs, and in so doing throws his head back and catches a glimpse of the moon through the last of the trees, and wandering near the edge of the road, trips over a broken cartwheel. His whole body tenses, and he whirls into a frenzy, swinging his stick about in the dark until he hits something. *Agghh! Coinneach!*

Agghh... you're just hit me in the mouth with that caber you right royal court jester... hellfire and damnation that hurts. They stagger out of the woods, laughing drunk.

See what you have made me do, you Highland hoodwinker, now I have nearly broken my shin on that thing... and staved my wrist into the bargain.

Mmm... Coinneach says, a hand in his mouth, *I think I may be losing a tooth soon.*

Stopping in the courtyard, Coinneach shows Andrew his reflection in the water of the horse trough. *Look at your injuries: left forearm, right cheek, and mine...* He shows his left hand where he caught a glancing blow and his mouth, from where blood dribbles down his left cheek.

Oh, prime pigswill Coinneach, that was not an attack, that was an accident, that was not what you said.

Well it was an attack for me, on me, actually, albeit a misdirected one, and what did you feel like at the exact moment itself? As if somebody had tripped you up?

Andrew thinks. *I suppose you are right, I might give you that or half give you that... what... what is it Coinneach, what?*

Coinneach is standing very still and serious, sober even, suddenly staring straight ahead into the darkness behind Andrew's head. Only a few feet away, a middle-aged woman with white hair, is staring at Coinneach, her lips mouthing some words without sound, then gradually she is fading back into the darkness, fading until, as Andrew finally spins around to look, she is gone altogether.

Is your mother's sister called Jeannie, Andrew?

Err.. one of them is, yes... why?

She has just died. Coinneach says and turns around, heading off into the barn to get to sleep.

What did you say, Coinneach?! That is not amusing, not humorous at all Coinneach... come back here and apologise!

Keep the noise down there! Someone shouts from the roofline, a light on at an opened window in the farmhouse above.

Chapter Six

Coinneach and the other farm hands are given a ride on a couple of carts over to the cottages at Muir of Ord. The divots are still being laid on the roof as they arrive.

As Coinneach is unpacking his few possessions from his rolled blanket, Màiri Chisholm rides up and greets him. *Have you seen Andrew Grant? Why is he not here today?* She seems slightly agitated.

Coinneach reaches up and calms her horse, stroking its head, squinting to look up, Màiri silhouetted against the morning sun. *He was called away, Màiri, he received word of an illness in his family.*

Well this is worse, then… his family have sent further news. It is a death now, the same woman I suppose- an aunt I think.

Coinneach nods his head. *Well he has probably reached them by now, he will know the sad news himself.*

Màiri starts to turn her horse, then shouts back to him: *My cousin Helen had twins…*

Begging your pardon, Ma'am?

My unexpected news, Coinneach, you said I would get unexpected news from a relative… We did not even know she was with child.

Good. He nods his head. *That is very agreeable, a blessing on your family… are the babes in sound health?*

Yes, they both are, I have seen them myself… they are full of life, she smiles warmly.

And how is your neck? He asks absentmindedly, looking off into the distance.

You know, it was fine until we spent the night, my father and I, in a millhouse on the way back from cousin Helen's. Our host had jammed the window open, and the damp air from the running stream nearby had given me cramp here by the morning. She rubs her neck.

Mmm... Coinneach smiles and nods a little, and looks about, beginning to lift some logs to take inside for the fireplace.

Was all that really in my palm?

No! He laughs, looking back up at her. *No, I made it all up. It is chance you are marvelling at there, just one of God's many wonders!*

~

The hired hands are digging in the fields, swinging pickaxes, stripped to the waist. When they rest, Andrew and Coinneach go over and sit on a turf dyke, looking down to where the new stair wing of Fairburn Tower is progressing up to first floor level. Andrew wipes the sweat from his face with his shirt and points down at the door: *Well Coinneach, you scared me off all right with your devilry there...*

Andrew, that is a phrase we would both do well to avoid using, even in idle conversation. Just last month two old footers over at Burghhead got arrested and tortured for mentioning Auld Nick in a quarrel, never mind enlisting his help. Have I not told you that second sight has a noble tradition in the Long Island?

Aye, and so has devilry for all I know. He throws his shirt down and stands up.

Coinneach doesn't rise to the bait, letting this slight on his forefathers go unchecked for the moment.

Just how did you get to know that about my mother's sister, Coinneach? Tell me how that is possible? He kneels down again angrily and thrusts his face into Coinneach's. *Please tell me how to reconcile that with my normal everyday view of God's creation?*

I saw her, Andrew. When people die, sometimes they travel to say farewell to their relatives. If you had been asleep and dreaming at that moment, then she might have entered your dream as a character to speak to you, or made your dream into one of her childhood memories to share with you. But you were awake and drunk, and I am sensitive to these things, so I saw her for you. She may even have wanted me tell you, to pass on the message.

What message? Andrew snorts.

It is often the same message I suppose. Goodbye, to know that you were important to her, that she thought of you, and she is happy now, that death is not so bad as you fear.

How could you know her name, when I had never spoken of her?

Her name was part of her, Andrew. When I say "see" in this situation I always also mean "know". I made her acquaintance one might say, however briefly.

Andrew shakes his head disbelievingly. *And this tower then, how do you "know" about this? Does this tower walk over to your bed of an evening and tip its hat to you, while its stair falls off onto the floor with a clang?*

No, now that is something else. I can feel the vibration of the collapse, especially because people are killed and injured. It is like a sound that I hear. Their distress sends waves out like ripples in a pool, both backwards and forwards in time.

You talk in the present, as if you see this happening now, as we speak?

Yes, I feel the past, present and future in much the same way, don't you? They are all like memories.

Then the future has already happened?

Well. It is already happening right now, I would express it like that, and always happening, forevermore.

Then it cannot be changed?

Coinneach shakes his head, muttering, as if to an unseen

companion: *They always choke on that thorn…*

What?

Andrew, for some people, perhaps most people, it is better not to know the answer to that question, perhaps best not even to ask it.

Then it is "no" then, is it not? He gets angry again. *Well, is it not?! Do not play games with me, Coinneach, as if I were a child and you are God or a messiah. You are a mortal man, flesh and blood, anyone can see that. And if you carry this knowledge, then so might any other man also bear its weight. The answer I seek is "no" then, is it not?*

Coinneach nods his head, slowly.

Thank you. Andrew snorts, then strides off.

~

In the cottages at Muir of Ord, the men sleep four to a room. While they slumber, Coinneach begins to toss and turn in his sleep. There is moonlight and the shadows of trees moving on the white timber- panelled walls, but now the light seems to change, becoming almost green, while the moving shadows seem to expand to fill the whole room.

Coinneach sees a little girl in a red shawl playing at the edge of a garden. Huge trees swirl above her. Behind her is a white cottage with a pathway lined with lavender bushes. She begins playing on the roadway itself, and Coinneach becomes more and more agitated. The sound of the wind in the trees grows louder and louder, but another sound seems to be building underneath it, almost like drums. Too late, the sound resolves itself into horses' hooves and a carriage rattles around the corner at enormous speed. The horses only have time for one neighing protest before the little girl is engulfed under the storm of their multiple hooves. Four horses mill her body like so much chaff and wheat as

Coinneach cries out in pain, thrashing his arms about, as if to tear down the curtains of perception, her cries piercing his mind, shaking his soul to its foundations.

Andrew and Jamie, now awake, grab his arms and pin him down, slapping his face to try to wake him up. Eventually his eyes open, only to bare the whites at first, then his pupils rotate down from his forehead, their gaze wild and frightened. His breathing is feverish and irregular.

By Christ, Coinneach, what ails you? Was that a nightmare or a fit? Are you sick, man?

His teeth chatter, and his whole body continues to shake. He speaks only with difficulty... *cottage... carriage... horses...*

Are you all right, Coinneach? Do you need a doctor?

He shakes his head violently, then slower: *No... I am all right... just need time...*

The men go back to bed but continue to be disturbed by the irregular and unnatural patterns of his breathing.

~

Chapter Seven

At ten o'clock in the morning, Màiri rides up to the cottage, then goes to knock on the door. She raps on the window and calls Coinneach's name, then tentatively lets herself inside.

To her surprise, he is not in bed, but wrapped in a grey blanket, sitting cross-legged on the floor, facing into the unlit fireplace.

Coinneach? She says, coming closer, and then kneeling to talk to him: *The men said you had some sort of fit, but would not consent for a physician to be sent for. What ails you? I can fetch Doctor MacArthur from Strathpeffer and be back in an hour.*

I will be fit for work... by early afternoon. He says quietly, not looking up, his eyes still fixed straight ahead. *You may tell your father not to fret as to the lost hours... I will work them on... or he can dock my wages... as he wishes.*

Coinneach... you do not seem yourself, what is the matter really? Sighing, she pulls up a chair. *I shall await my answer... as long as it takes.*

Finally his eyes come back into focus, and he laughs a little, looks up at her: *I had a bad dream, Màiri Chisholm... like a silly little boy. I had a bad dream.*

Andrew tells me you saw a vision of his aunt, at the hour of her death. He says you have foreseen that there will be an accident at Fairburn Tower this season. This dream you have just had was more than just a dream was it not, Coinneach?

He stands up and goes to throw water over his head. Màiri recoils and averts her eyes, goes to stand at the door while he pulls on a vest and breeches. After a few minutes, he emerges, sniffing the air. *Right then, shall we go together?*

Go where? Màiri asks, startled.

To see my dream, or its setting at least. It concerns a place not far from here. You shall be my witness to this. I can walk, or we can take your horse.

You can ride well? She asks, blushing a little.

He nods his head.

Oh Coinneach, it would be improper for us to be seen abroad like that together, you must know that.

He laughs aloud, *I know, I know, I was only teasing you. I will go and borrow one from the neighbours. They are my friends already, since I told them that their son will grow up to be a school teacher.*

And will he? She exclaims, spinning around.

I really don't have the vaguest idea, Coinneach shrugs, *but for now it gets me the use of a horse, does it not?*

Oh Coinneach. She shakes her head, clucking.

~

After two or three miles Màiri and Coinneach arrive at a white cottage on a bend in the road and dismount, tethering their horses.

Here, Coinneach says, framing the view with his hands, *this is what I saw...*

Màiri stands next to him, the closest she has stood, looking for a second at his sightless eye, the way the eyelid rests half-shut over it, the curious dark texture of his skin. It is as if he is always half-sleeping, she thinks to herself, peaceful but haunted, like a sleepwalker in a waking world.

The wind blows in these trees with enormous energy... He flutters his hands around his head, *making lots of noise, like the sea it is so loud, then the horses come running around the bend and she cannot hear their hooves...*

Who cannot?

The little girl with the red shawl, who plays in this garden. And what happens to her?

She goes under the hooves and they trample her to death, a carriage and horses goes over her.

Oh that is horrible... horrible... Màiri says, looking down at her feet.

You think so? Coinneach asks. *Horrible to hear of it? I had to watch it. I felt it. I felt the hooves hit her, I was inside her body...*

Oh please, please don't, Coinneach... Màiri turns away.

Màiri, he touches her shoulder, catching her, *I even felt what the horses feel: it hurts them too, it panics them. And there is a driver somewhere... on the carriage, and a passenger inside with a gold chain, shining boots. And also... the child's mother is nearby... her emotion is like a background to all this, it is like a wave about to break. I cannot bear that... that is when I woke up... her pain, her fear and horror are unbearable to me.*

Màiri looks at him, her eyes full of pity. She places her hand on his shoulder. *Coinneach, have you had many experiences like this before?*

My whole wretched life, and it does not get any easier.

What did people say when you told them of things like this, on Lewis, in the other places you have worked?

Why do you think I keep moving, Màiri? People are horrified that a man should foresee something, then doubly horrified when it comes to pass. In a strange sort of way you can become associated with the event. People can blame you, as if you might even have brought it about somehow.

So what shall we do? She asks.

Nothing. He sighs, preparing to re-mount his horse. *At least then nobody will blame me.*

Except me. Màiri says indignantly. *You have to warn that girl's mother, we have to find her and tell her.*

Màiri, he says, leaning his face closer, *believe me when I tell you this: that the future cannot be changed and only fools will try.*

But you have got to try, Coinneach, how do you know it is not possible? Who have you tried to save in the past? How can you be so certain? Perhaps it is only difficult but not impossible. You are a coward...

This makes him stop, one foot in the stirrup, he turns back. *Màiri...* he points a finger at his own temple, *with this faculty, a coward would be driven to take his own life. It takes fortitude just to live, to wake, to sleep, when you have seen the future and how much suffering it holds for humankind.*

To love? she asks, wiping a tear from her eye.

What?

She turns and mounts her horse, and they both canter towards home. *To love, I said, Coinneach. Have you ever dared to love somebody? Ever dared to step outside that invisible suit of armour you wear and really be a human being? Or do you just observe and hold your breath and horde all your little secrets?*

You know so little about me. He shakes his head.

Enlighten me, then.

If I am lacking in compassion for my fellows then why did this premonition make me so ill? I love the little girl, even though I have never met her. I love her and I hate what happens to her.

Then why not try to save her?

Because I do not believe that is possible.

And what about women? Have you never met one that you wanted to make your wife, or at least to kiss?

Coinneach laughs. *I am a normal man in most respects, of course I feel those things from time to time. But if I cannot make a thing better then I leave it alone. Who would benefit from any kind of union with an unnatural creature like me?*

Now she notices his sly smile and sees that he might be

jousting with her. *I wonder if you mean any of that...?* She says then unfurls her whip, sitting up in her saddle. *I should go now. I will tell my father that you have made a fine recovery and will be at work again at the farm after noon. Coinneach, tell me when is it that you forecast this little girl is to meet her horrible demise?*

I am not certain... at least a couple of months from now... perhaps autumn. I saw some of the leaves were on the ground. You won't speak of any of this to your father, will you?

Coinneach, I will tell him you are the prophet Elijah unless you promise to come with me to that woman's house some evening soon, whereupon we shall warn her of your prophecy.

Reluctantly, their horses now facing in opposite directions, Coinneach nods his head, and she holds out her hand to shake his. For a second his heart melts as he feels its softness enclosed within his own, then she gallops away and he continues homeward.

~

Chapter Eight

Under a grey sky spitting with rain, the men work at the side of a millpond, renewing its mossy walls, some of them with their legs in the water. A sudden rumbling sound is heard, then a crash and distant voices, shockwaves pass across the surface of the water under their eyes. Most of the men stop work, then head towards the hilltop, some starting to run. Coinneach just sighs and sits down to rest next to the millwheel, staring absent-mindedly into the water.

In a few minutes one of the men returns, his voice raised excitedly: *It's the castle, Fairburn Tower. There's been some kind of accident. They're shouting for a doctor… men are trapped.*

Andrew looks at Coinneach: *You knew didn't you? Did you know it would be this day?*

Coinneach shrugs and shakes his head, ducking the question. *There's not much else would make that sort of a noise, short of cannon fire.*

Everyone downs tools now and begin to run towards the scene, but Coinneach moves sluggishly. Andrew notices this and is angered by it: *Do you not want to help, man? You could have been the first there, pulling them out?*

A second rumble sounds now, and more stones slide down. Now within sight: a cloud of dust billows out from the base of the tower, voices rising in confusion. Andrew looks back at Coinneach accusingly: *So I suppose you knew that into the bargain, and have just saved us all broken arms?*

Coinneach shrugs and raises his hands in a gesture of hopelessness. *Look, let us just do some good now shall we? Not apportion blame for providence like fools on a sinking boat?*

They reach the base of the rubble and begin ferrying

stones away, some bloodied arms and hands gesturing, muted cries coming clear as the gang gradually free them, carrying bodies out onto the grass nearby, dust wiping across the sky and fields until an eerie silence begins to settle again, soon to be filled with the arrival of horses' hooves, the wailing of women.

~

In the evening Màiri sends a messenger with a note for Coinneach, and he is relieved to have a reason to leave the oppressive atmosphere at the cottage, the men talking about the Fairburn accident while Andrew swallows his tongue; all the time wanting to mention Coinneach's prophecy, but aware that it might go down badly while wounded men are struggling for their lives. Coinneach says as he leaves that he has been called to the farmhouse to discuss his wages and overtime, surprised to find himself reluctant to mention Màiri's name.

He arrives at the white cottage with the lavender bushes, as the summer sun re-emerges over the fields. Màiri waves from the door of the house with a small white-haired woman at her side. She introduces them: *Coinneach, this is Helen MacPherson, I have told her about your premonition and she wanted to meet you. She believes in the second sight and is interested to hear what you have to say, especially in light of today's dreadful events at Fairburn.*

Is it true? The old lady asks excitedly, *That you foresaw that? That is so uncanny! Is there any news of the poor souls involved?*

They sit down with her at her table in a dark, modestly furnished room. Coinneach's eyes flicker over every surface, keenly attentive to the surroundings, even before she begins speaking.

My children are grown up now, Mister Mackenzie, there is none of them that fits the description in your dream as Miss Chisholm has described it to me. I can warn all my neighbours if you wish, some of them have young children but they seldom play on my land. What would you advise me to do?

Coinneach reaches into his jerkin pocket and withdraws a grey circular stone and holds it before them in the palm of his hand, and lies: *This is a keepsake from my Mother in Lewis, God rest her soul, she told me it was given to her by a Norwegian princess. I carry it everywhere…*

But what…? The old lady is puzzled.

I sometimes use it to focus my thoughts, to help me remember my premonitions, to see them again more clearly. If you will take my hand then with the other one I will raise this stone to my eye and meditate again upon what I saw.

Coinneach looks at the stone and runs his finger over its carved surface, the incised decoration, casting his mind back into the state of shock when the stone first saved his life: on the moors above Uig Bay. He blinks his good eye and in his mind his blind eye re-awakens. Eye and stone become one to him, a portal between death and life, dreams and waking. He drifts back down through layers of consciousness, softly falling, as if through autumn leaves. He clutches the woman's hand and the dream begins again: the child playing, the sun on the lavenders, the wind in the trees. This time he hears a voice calling to her, and he tries to move closer into the mind of the girl: *Fiona or Flora…* he mutters.

Why… that is my little niece's name… Flora… you don't think?

Coinneach is trying to stay down, to move sideways from her mind to see where she lives, but the women's voices are disturbing him now. Feeling the horses' hooves approaching again, he brings himself back up to the surface, starting to shake again, shivering. The women fetch a blanket to put around him, place a bowl of hot broth into his hands.

She has a niece, Coinneach, called Flora, who often comes to visit here in the summer, in August. That will be who you see?

Perhaps... Coinneach says, nodding his head, his expression still distant.

Well, it is straightforward then, Màiri says. *We can write to her, tell her not to visit this year. You could go to visit her instead, could you not Mrs MacPherson?*

Well, I am not so sprightly as once I was, but yes I suppose my son could travel with me.

There then! Màiri smiles, folding her hands on her lap. *The thing is settled, a calamity averted.*

Helen MacPherson looks straight ahead at Coinneach whose face is still vacant, his gaze miles away. *I don't think your sweetheart is so convinced as you.*

Och! Màiri laughs, touching the old woman's shoulders. *Do not call Coinneach that! He is a friend, an employee of my father. You will be spreading untruths with language like that.*

Spread the story about the corner and the horses, Coinneach finally says. *If you want to try to be safe, then tell everyone in this hamlet about my premonition, and have your son cut back that thicket so that the bend in the road is not so blind. You could do these things if you wish.*

There! Màiri says, as they leave the house. *Now how was that for bravery? You may have saved a life tonight, Coinneach. You should speak out more about these visions of yours, then people will be grateful for your gift, so they will not curse you as a witch.*

And is that what they are doing now, about Fairburn? Coinneach spins around.

No. Why? Màiri seems taken aback.

You told that woman I had foretold the accident, which seemed to fair thrill her, but I wonder if the Laird of Fairburn will find it so appealing?

Oh, Coinneach, why do you live in the shadows so? Come out into the sunlight with the rest of us, or even... Màiri lifts her hand to the half-moon rising, *...into the moonlight?*

He says nothing, but looks down at the dusty road.

Come on, it is late, I will give you a ride back to Ord, since I see you have no horse. Jump up.

As they ride back under the treetops then out over the twilight moor, he feels her body close to his and knows of course that this is what she wants him to feel. Unlike him, Màiri can only guess at the thoughts of others, but knows that the taste of her long brown hair blowing into his face must be something as sacred to a man as any spell or prayer, as bewitching as a dream.

This knowledge is in her body, Coinneach thinks, like the grace that makes women move so much more fluidly than men, the grace of horses and birds in flight. He notices her earrings and bracelets, such as women must have worn since the dawn of time; and thinks how they are celebrations of themselves, as needful and revelatory to the world as flowers, while dumb impoverished men scuttle over the earth like crabs, hard and avid, bent on war.

What are you thinking? She asks very gently, as they draw near to the cottages and dismount, hoping not to be heard.

Suddenly, a gust of wind goes through Coinneach's head and takes everything clever or guarded right out of it, and he is alarmed to find himself leaning close to her, to smell her face and hair again, saying sadly: *How very beautiful you are...* He listens to the words left on the air and is quite surprised to recognise them as his own voice, and they suddenly cut him. He sobs, and she runs a hand down his cheek and a huge tear rolls to meet it there, and they kiss in the darkness, her breath moving into his.

~

Chapter Nine

The men are digging, widening the mill race, while nearby the joiners cut wood for a new mill wheel, forming it on its side on the ground. While Coinneach breaks rocks, sweating, Andrew and Jamie are exchanging gossip with the joiners as they work: *So what's the Laird saying to the demise of his new stair tower then?*

The word is he is to compensate the families of the injured and perished by confiscating the house and lands of the principal mason...

That sounds a mite severe on the mason. How so does he blame the man?

He has appointed an architect now who says that insufficient foundations were laid for such soft clay. An elementary mistake he calls it... so he is resolved to have the shirt off the mason's back now.

And what were the labourers getting quizzed about yesterday?

Och... there is a daft rumour going around that some local farm hand predicted the whole thing, and the works foremen want to find him and see what else he had knowledge of...

Andrew and Jamie stop work and look at each other, laughing nervously.

What? The joiners look up.

They turn to look at Coinneach, who stops, wiping his face on his forearm.

You are looking at him, gentlemen, Andrew announces in mock-aristocratic tones, *may we present to you our esteemed local soothsayer Coinneach Odhar...* They applaud and laugh some more, then sadden a little, remembering the recent loss of life.

The joiners smile uncertainly, looking at everybody else's expressions, while Coinneach just goes back to work without comment, face blank, swinging the hammer harder than ever.

~

Working in the heat of the midday sun, one of a gang of about twenty to thirty men stripped to the waist, Coinneach sees a carriage with elaborate livery drawing up at the gateway to the Fairburn Lands. One carriage wheel sticks in a rut, and the footman tries and fails to shift it with a pike, then turns and gesticulates for help.

With their shirts back on for modesty's sake, the men go over and lean-to as the carriage's contents- a group of well-to-do young ladies - all dismount to lighten the load and snigger at the roadside from behind their lace shawls and twisting parasols.

The carriage righted, Coinneach and the others bow deferentially in gratitude for a scattering of coins, then return across the furrows. *What cargo were they then?* Coinneach asks.

The Earl of Cromartie's children, Coinneach, on a visit to Laird Roderick Mackenzie of Fairburn, the finest future young ladies of the land.

Coinneach snorts. *Only flesh and blood, however, are they not? God does not label the fruit upon his trees.*

No indeed, nor the neeps in his furrows I dare say, Jamie laughs.

Getting ideas above your station, Coinneach? Andrew chips in: *now that is the sort of prophecy we would all like to hear! Farm labourer to wed aristocrat's daughter!*

Or even a farm manager's daughter? Jamie asks, leadingly.

Leave off, Jamie. Coinneach says.

What's this, James. Do you know something?

~

Later as they all head home along the road, the sun at a softer angle, the carriage passes again and Coinneach looks up to see a slim black-haired girl, of perhaps nine or ten, staring out at him, her elbows on the carriage door, her chin rested at a bored, wistful angle. Something strikes him like a hammer blow, and her black eyes bore into him, something strangely predatory in her stare. The gaze echoes and expands for a second; a wave of terror passes through him. He walks on more slowly afterwards, deep in thought, shaken.

As he lags behind, Andrew falls back to accompany him. *What troubles you, Coinneach? You have grown as pale as a ghost, if one might dare to use such an expression in your uncanny presence.*

I have just seen something, Andrew... someone... who I think may be from my future. One of those girls, the little Cromartie ladies, I think she will grow up to be my downfall somehow, my destroyer.

Andrew senses he is serious, and desists from his recent brand of humour. *Well, it is possible, Coinneach. As we saw last week, the lairds of these lands can still have any of us flogged on a whim, so it would seem little changes from one generation to the next. We should wait and pay great attention to see whom they each marry, then stay well clear of their parishes - what do you say?*

He puts his arm around his friend's shoulder for a moment, but as they pass the Ord Tavern a group of joiners lean out and raise their flagons, shouting: *Coinneach Odhar Mackenzie, hail the great seer, well met, man!*

~

Màiri and her father pull up outside the cottages in a horse and cart. Andrew greets them, already dressed in black, and they confer for a moment, looking up towards the window, from where Coinneach looks out.

Irritated, Màiri leaves the men there and hurries up to the house, her long black dress brushing over the wild flowers that line the flagstone pathway. She knocks on the door and leans in, almost whispering: *Coinneach, good day to you. Will you not come to the burial of those two poor souls who perished at Fairburn? It is a sign of respect!*

Màiri... he says, *please let no one be offended, least of all yourself, but I try to avoid burials as oft as I can. I cannot recall ever exchanging a word with either of these men so my farewell would only perplex them.*

Is there more behind this? She asks.

Graveyards trouble me Màiri, to you they may be quiet places, but to me they are full of voices.

Oh Coinneach! She raises her gloved hands to her head in exasperation. *Can you not be ordinary even for a morning?*

She flutters away like a black bird from the doorway, and Coinneach follows to stand and wave after them, as Andrew and Jamie and some of the other labourers jump up onto the back of the cart.

Coinneach sits down on the doorstep, and takes his divining stone out, turning it over in his hand, his brow troubled, peering into its centre.

~

Chapter Ten

Andrew and Coinneach down tools at midday, and walk to the well together, putting on their shirts. *Coinneach, that woman has feelings for you, I am certain of it, you should be honoured, she is a gentle dove.*

And you speak of...?

Oh, don't play your games, Coinneach. Andrew retorts, then looking about and speaking more quietly, adds: *Màiri, of course.*

I know, Andrew, Coinneach sighs, running his hands through his hair, *but it cannot be.*

They stand and take turns to douse themselves in water at the stoup. *Why ever not?* Andrew asks, *You could yet make something of yourself, you are as astute as any merchant or manager I have ever met with. We need not till the soil forever.*

I will not marry her, because somebody else will. I have looked into the future and seen this, that my destiny lies elsewhere.

Oh Conn... this will be that stone that Màiri told me about. Why do you not throw it into the sea and take some pleasure for yourself? An old cold stone will not keep you warm or content through a Highland winter.

Jamie suddenly joins them, out of breath: *...the manager says everyone is called over to Fairburn presently... just leave your tools where you are... there is to be an assembly at the Tower.*

~

When they get there, various gentlemen in fine coats and starched stockings are already addressing the crowd on a temporary wooden stage at the foot of Fairburn Tower:

...Mistakes were made, and the accounts have been settled in that regard, and I may say the Laird has done right by you and has taken good care of the affected families, out of Christian compassion, it is true, but also as an ongoing signal of his determination to bring this project to completion before this summer ends, and to retain the energy of all you fine young men...

At this a toothless old man in the crowd laughs aloud, his fellows slapping his bare back.

...And to line your pockets handsomely in the process...

At this a universal cheer goes up.

And... and... -The orator struggles to be heard, *...And in this regard I am authorised to issue revised rates this season, of six shillings a week until the new Stair Tower is completed. What do you all say?*

As a second cheer subsides, Coinneach turns to go, but the next words make him halt: *...And now while some of you sign up for this, the Laird has asked me that the man known as Coinneach Odhar be brought forward, as some of you may have heard, this fellow is reputed to have shown an uncanny gift of prophecy regarding the fate of Fairburn Tower.*

Reluctantly, as more and more people turn to look at him, Coinneach sees that he has no choice, and makes his way slowly towards the front, some friends slapping him on the back.

Please... come up, Coinneach, -The gentleman speaks softly, offering his handshake, and gesturing to his companions on the stage. *This is the architect Charles Cameron from Edinburgh and his new head mason Neal Faichney.*

The architect addresses him in English at first, and then the mason takes over in Gaelic: *Is it true, sir, that you foresaw the unfortunate collapse at the tower and told some witnesses among your friends?*

Yes sir, I did.

And what precisely did your vision show you and how did you come by this talent?

My vision showed me the stair tower falling down in rubble, as it reached the mid second storey, and men's bloodied arms and hands stretching from between the fallen stones for the assistance of their fellows. I saw that it was a lightly raining day, with a dark grey cloud perched over Ben Wyvis, about midday.

Astonishing... and did you divine the cause of the collapse, sir?

Only vaguely... I foresaw the face of the head mason as the event happened, and the fear in his youthful heart. I saw something hidden there, a doubt that he had not ordered the ground to be prepared sufficiently, a fear that he would be discovered and condemned for this oversight.

And why, Coinneach, did you not come forward to us, or to your own foreman, with this premonition?

Sir, I have been in this parish but a season: I hail from the Lews. I feared that no man would take my words seriously, or worse still that the head mason himself would have me jailed for slander against his profession.

The well-dressed gentlemen nod to each other, and the architect passes another question to be translated:

Coinneach, how do you see into the future, and what can you tell us about the future now of Fairburn Tower?

At this, Coinneach pauses for a second, looks down and then turns to address the crowd directly, and lifts his grey stone out from his pocket and holds it up for everyone to see. He raises his voice with sudden and surprising confidence, and the architect, fascinated, presses his aide to translate for him.

This is the seer stone my mother gave me in the land of my birth, the Isle of Lewis, given to her by the ghost of a Viking queen buried in the local churchyard. She was told that it would bestow upon her son Coinneach the gift of second sight!

Now with this stone, I can see into the future, I can divine the fates of generations yet to be born in this land, your children and grandchildren, people whom you will never see but who nonetheless shall be your blood descendants. These people, when their time comes upon this earth, will marvel at my predictions and their accuracy, because you will have handed them down to them in story, in legend and song, as part of tradition itself. Therefore note well what I say now and teach it to all those who come after, so that the people of the future will know that we saw into their lives, that their fates were known to us, and that the human mind is more miraculous than any art or science can describe, that the human soul can transcend the body.

Work hard, labour well for now on Fairburn Tower, for this project will now pass happily, and no further harm shall befall those who toil here...

A cheer goes up, and the educated men confer excitedly.

This castle shall be thronged with rich and powerful guests and its halls shall ring loud with notes of music and laughter... however...

Incredibly, a cloud crosses the sun at this moment, and the coincidence is lost on no-one, heads turned by its suddenness. The seer continues:

...Ere several generations have passed, the day will come when the Mackenzies of Fairburn shall lose their entire possessions, and that branch of the clan shall disappear almost to a man from the face of the earth. Their castle shall become uninhabited, desolate and forsaken, and a cow shall give birth to a calf in the uppermost chamber of the ruins of Fairburn Castle.

As Coinneach speaks, he finds the stone gives him strength, creates a calm about and within him somehow. He sees further than before, as if the whole crowd see with him, are inadvertently amplifying his power. New images play out across his sight: the Tower ages and decays in fast-forward, its roof disappearing, it begins falling down, moss and grass advancing up its ramparts, stones falling away, as all the time light and dark flicker over it as clouds race and seasons change. He sees wealthy people in strange black Victorian costumes travelling in strings of horseless carriages from Inverness and Edinburgh and London, just to climb the tower and marvel at the cow with her calf. He hears them saying his name, recounting the words of his prophecy. This knowledge amplifies his sight, permanently weakens the walls of time around him. He feels a rush of exhilaration.

Silence has fallen over the crowd, as Coinneach lowers the stone, and looks out over all the faces, then turns to see the dignitaries, their amazed stares, their open mouths.

Eventually, the chairman pulls himself together and shakes Coinneach's hand: *Thank you, sir, I don't think that any of us have ever heard anything quite like that, although I would perhaps urge you not to speak of some of it in the presence of the Laird himself if you should ever meet him.*

Is that likely? Coinneach asks, almost laughing.

Sir, if you can truly do what you say you can, then the King himself will want an audience.

And his enemies pursue me.

The chairman stops in his tracks at this, and leans closer: *I think I see that you are a keen-witted fellow indeed, no child with a toy, eh, Coinneach? You will need all of that cunning to preserve yourself from the jealousy of men if you continue thus... mark well my words.*

Now the crowd are clapping, and the effect spreads, as if a spell has been broken. Coinneach bows modestly to them, and then departs the stage.

~

Chapter Eleven

Màiri, Andrew and Coinneach, well-dressed, leave the Kirk together and take their Sunday afternoon walk across the open moors, occasionally passing others whom they know, or stopping to admire the view.

Coinneach, I spoke to Helen Macpherson last week before she left. She has set off with her son for Oban, to visit her niece Flora. She has warned everyone in her village about your dream. Now the accident cannot happen. We have changed the future, you and I. Are you not glad?

He stops and sighs and looks at her: *I am glad that these things bring you happiness Màiri, but I fear that fate is not so easily re-negotiated as Mrs Macpherson's summer itinerary.*

You have been morose of late, my friend, Andrew says, *you spend too much time meditating with that stone of yours. What has it told you?*

Coinneach sits down on a boulder, to look out across the moors towards the clear water of the Cromarty Firth, waves tinged grey-brown where they melt into the mudflats of Dingwall.

I have seen that men will invent carriages of metal that move at great speed, powered by invisible flames, that require no horses. (Cars speed past behind them on a tarmac road, silver and red blurs, snatches of music blowing from their stereos). Màiri turns her head, and the dirt track is quiet again, her hair blowing across her eyes.

I have seen that a new loch will be made above Beauly, but that the water will overflow and flood the valley below (in 1967, heavy rain causes the hydroelectric dam at Torachilty to overflow, flooding the village of Conon Bridge: a flash of foam seeps across a part of the view in front of Coinneach).

Oh yes, he says, pointing over his head, *and giant grey geese, built of metal, will howl and roar across the sky* (a passenger jet begins its descent towards Inverness Airport; two RAF tornadoes hurtle by on their way out to manoeuvres over the Dornoch Firth). Andrew lifts his head, and only a squadron of living geese pass by, beginning their late summer departure for the south.

And all across the high moors of the Highlands I see plantations of turning white crosses, strange unmanned windmills higher than castles (a windfarm appears on the right shoulder of Ben Wyvis, gleaming as white as the snow-filled corries).

Who will you tell? Màiri asks. *You could have the ear of kings with such powers, become as wealthy as any laird.*

He shakes his head and flicks his stone over in his hand. *No, I have done the most difficult thing of all now. What happened at Fairburn gave me the strength to attempt it. I have turned the stone on myself and divined my own future… and now I know what needs to be done.*

They both turn to look at him expectantly, but Màiri's turn of her head brings into view a distant figure waving on the road, running to meet them. *Wait a moment…* she says, and rises to walk towards the messenger.

Coinneach stares straight ahead, smiling sadly to himself and says: *You had better go with her, Andrew.*

Andrew picks himself up and catches a last phrase as he turns:

…and take good care of her.

The phrase lodges in his head as he catches up with the small group and sees that Màiri has tears in her eyes, saying something about a child trampled under a coach and horses, how a doctor has to be called, the woman is hysterical and breathless.

Returning to tell Coinneach, Andrew finds the whole wide moor mysteriously empty, as if his friend had never existed. Some gulls wheel overhead, their cries mocking him as he calls out after Coinneach, as if they know, as if they've taken him. He throws a stone up at them in empty rage, then runs back towards the road.

~

Chapter Twelve

Even a Seer cannot achieve a dematerialisation. Coinneach is running now as fast as he can along a dried river bed, sweat on his face merging with tears in his eyes, his heart racing as he pushes himself ever further, trying to vanish out of life, to become pure blood, only feeling, no thought, no past, no regret.

He will stop eventually, and drink from a stream, but continue walking west until nightfall, then arise with daybreak and begin again.

He crosses the country, drawn to the rugged west coast, the stinging sea, the endless islands of his birth. He lifts his eyes to the sun and the sky and the glens, and lets the landscapes fall into him. The ever-changing cloudscapes wipe his mind clean, the cruel rocks and precipices cut and re-cut him; a diamond to refract the light, he falls on his back on moors, cushioned by heather, and light plays in his eyes, dazzling, hypnotic. Always he arises again, and keeps moving.

He remembers the loneliness of his childhood, his frequent flight from the jeers and accusations of others. Here he is always at one again: enfolded in the shapeless spirit that creates and destroys all things. He walks on its earth, he serves it, he worships it with his soul, honing himself like a knife. *What do you want of me?* He asks of it, his heart open like a sacrifice, yelling into the wind.

Gaining the high slopes above Strathcarron, he catches sight of the glittering sea lochs, the fortress of Applecross, the Cuillins melting like ice in the steaming ocean. And the landscape answers him: that this ever-receding horizon that beckons and blossoms like a girl's face, is a beautiful alluring stranger, drawing him on. It commands of him to live and love without hope of return, taking everything on trust, to burn in the sun until he is consumed by it, and never to turn back.

~

In Lochcarron, he finds the story of his Fairburn prophecy has already spread, carried by itinerant Gaels like himself, returning west, and shocked to see his wind-torn appearance; people give him fresh clothes and food. They ask him for his stories, but first he insists that they tell theirs. For hours he absorbs their local clan histories , the legends they tell their children about nearby landmarks. He finds he is becoming a celebrity now, and young and old reach out to touch him.

Every touch is like a spark of flame: lighting up some strange black tree buried within him; he looks off into the shadows behind a child's face and sees a whole cascade of generations reaching upward and away like sea cliffs, built on this foundation. He finds he is part of life, no longer alone, the hopes and fears of all his people move into him like the waves of the sea, nourished by their language and song.

In return, he points to the long shore of the far side of the loch, and sketches with his hands and words the spectre of an iron horse, black and belching steam, howling like a banshee, drawing a long line of carriages behind it, all the way from London to Inverness then along their shore and on to the Isle of Skye.

~

Around the headland at Kishorn, he senses something even stranger, and sits for many hours among the bracken on the hillside with his divining stone, staring in wonder out into the loch, trying to unravel the meaning of what he senses.

Finally he returns to the shore, and as the sun sets he dazzles the villagers with his dreamlike tale: *a one-legged monster made of metal will rise here, and then go twice beneath the water, breathing fire, and the third time will spell disaster in the German Ocean* (the Kishorn oil rig workers assemble the Ninian Central Platform behind him in the deep water, in the 1970s, the largest mobile structure on earth, the only one-legged oil-rig built, tested twice by full submersion in the water, its oil flare burning 24 hours a day, struck at sea by a submarine in March 1988. Piper Alpha explodes in July 1988).

Children delight in the story of the fire-breathing monster, but there are other shapes he sees looming out of the darkness. There is a shadow falling soon over all of the Highlands he thinks, a foreign spectre of false hopes who will land in the west and march on Edinburgh and London. He senses disastrous defeat in battle, then a time of great trial, centuries of desolation, people driven from their homes. He wants to warn them, but knows he has not seen enough detail, the picture is incomplete. With a heavy heart, withholding this knowledge, he embraces them each in turn the next morning, before setting out for the north.

~

Coinneach walks into Shieldaig, and the distant past pours over him. He sits down on a boulder and gazes through his stone. Strange voices and accents emerge from the woods. He sees the Norsemen centuries earlier, dragging their longships overland, across the bogs beneath Beinn Eighe and Liathach, overland from Loch Maree. He marvels at the spectacle of the ropes and the chanting men, the chainmail, the gleaming axes, domed helmets, their fine women in the furs of strange beasts, the lit fires on the shore, ale drunk from intricate carved horns.

His reverie is interrupted: the curious villagers have come to look at him, timid and peaceful as if he is some exotic fish washed ashore. They reach out to touch his seer-stone as he explains its powers.

The same pattern is repeated: they give him food, shelter for the night, and share their stories with him, the tales of the exploits of their forebears. He helps them to see the Norsemen again in their imaginations, is shown faces, red and blonde haired children, imposing jaws and foreheads, and they laugh at the traces in their blood of these vanished men, wonder at what unions gave rise to them, the unknown stories.

Next morning he walks with them over the hills, around to Torridon, where something catches his eye. He raises his stone like a musket, and the villagers gasp in awe. In his vision, a huge scree slope on the mountain across the water slides down with a mighty crash, annihilating the village beneath. *How many generations?* They ask. *When will this come to pass?* The far future, he says, many generations, after the horseless carriages run over the grey ribbons from Inverness.

~

In Loch Broom he takes a little longer to draw attention to himself. Asking about catching a boat over to Lewis, he casually mentions the huge metal ship without sails that will cross the Minch four times a day between Loch Broom and Stornoway. The fishermen listen, puzzled, sceptical at first, until he grabs a few of their hands and quickly delves into the darkness behind their faces, tells them details of their homes, what fish they caught last week. A few of them even seem frightened by this, stepping backwards, although only some of it is divined, much of it guesswork. He sees that fear is stronger in them, the swell of the sea a terrible grey curtain that drives them daily into the bosom of the church.

Yes, he says, answering words in their heads before they are even voiced. *Such marvels as will sound like the work of the devil. The generations of the future, it pains me to relate, will be strange and godless, the people will degenerate as the land improves, I see ministers without grace and women without shame,* take care that your own children and grandchildren stay close to God and may still be numbered with the saved.

And what will become of this great metal ship that swallows horseless carriages? They ask.

When the name painted on its bow is The Isle of Lewis, then it will sink into the sea.

~

He reaches Lochinver, then onto Clachtoll Bay, the place of the hole in the rock. This curious symmetry appeals to him: he stands on the glowing blonde beach beneath the natural arch in the cliffs, and lifts his own holed-stone up before it. A resonance opens up. While all else remains calm round about, within the halo of the stone the cliff collapses, the vision expanding in ripples, rock exploding into the sea with a deafening roar, shaking the very core of the earth underfoot.

He turns around to address the villagers gathered behind him in curiosity: *This great stone arch, a portal forged by the sea, will be reclaimed by it ere many generations have passed, the crash it makes then will be so loud that the Laird of Leadmore's cattle, though Leadmore be twenty miles hence, shall break their tethers in fright* (in 1841, the arch collapses on a day when the Laird of Leadmore's cattle have escaped and wandered all the way to the clifftops above Clachtoll. The noise frightens them so much that they charge all the twenty miles home, leaving a trail of damage in their wake).

His audience lead him up to see the ruined broch, the iron-age dyke of sharp flagstones driven into the turf, the white luminous brown and unearthly green waves of Stoer Bay. The Seer sighs and breathes the layers of history in, the rush of the waves whispering of grey eternity. He feels the chill of autumn and winter in the air. The broch rebuilds itself behind him, peat smoke curling out of its monstrous funnel, leaking brown into the milky sky. He sees the ancient people and their cattle, feels the rough texture of their cloth on their skins, hidden within as ships pass on the horizon; first Roman galleys then Viking longships. Further back he finds the mind and hand of the Pictish engineer who travelled these coasts for decades, drawing his designs in the sand, given supreme authority by their new leader, uniting their kingdom for the first time in the face of the perceived threat: the Latin men with their armour and forts and palisades who drove them into the woods at Mons Graupius, but faltered, unwilling to follow them into the sacred kingdom of their Gods, hushed and green and dark.

~

He travels again, across vast moorlands where life itself seems to falter, only occasional eagles circle overhead in their unfathomable orbits. For days, the sun rises and re-animates his bones from cold stone. He rolls out of a sheepskin, and looks upon another infinite array of harsh rocks reaching into the bleak heart of his country. In every hamlet and township he passes, he sees the terrible future hand of exodus brush across, driving the people into the sea, westwards to far lands as yet unnamed in the western ocean. *The clans will become so effeminate as to flee from their native country before an army of sheep.*

Behind them in his visions: the sheep advance, the deer also, then again the strange fields of giant white crosses turning in the wind, and something else: he sees further than ever before; a terrible darkness moving over the sky for months, a rain of black ash that extinguishes all life.

Like fragments of a puzzle, the visions are still jumbled in his head sometimes, their order in time uncertain. He has much to study, to unravel, to divine the larger events that will give meaning to his vignettes.

~

He walks down into Loch Eriboll, the wild northern coast opening up before him. At last he feels as if he has the measure of his country.

The walls of the glen have a dark uncanny quality to them. He sits among the strewn rocks on the shore and wonders at the mute high faces of the cliffs, why they refuse to talk to him. He gazes through his divining-stone and senses that the secret on this place's lips is hidden beneath the dark water.

In time, a villager on the opposite shore begins to row a small white boat towards him, and he raises a hand to greet him.

Crossing the water, the Seer nearly loses his stone from his hands: as German U-boats begin to erupt through the water's surface on either side, rocking the small boat, dousing him in spray. The grey conning towers with strange insignia come first, then the greater bulk of the submarines themselves. The Seer cries out in alarm, and the boatman tries to calm him lest his thrashing arms capsize the boat.

74

The loch becomes a mass of these devilish sea monsters, and uniformed men emerge from the back of them, speaking a strange harsh language, arms raised or clasped behind their heads, as English-sounding soldiers pour onto the shore to meet them from their wagons, rifles and bayonets at the ready.

The boatman throws Coinneach onto the shore, and leans over him, pinning his arms: *What ails you man? You nearly sank us, are you sick or possessed by devils?*

A war will end here… Coinneach gasps, spitting imaginary water from his lungs, *a great war that will sweep the whole earth, it will end here… and I have seen it.*

~

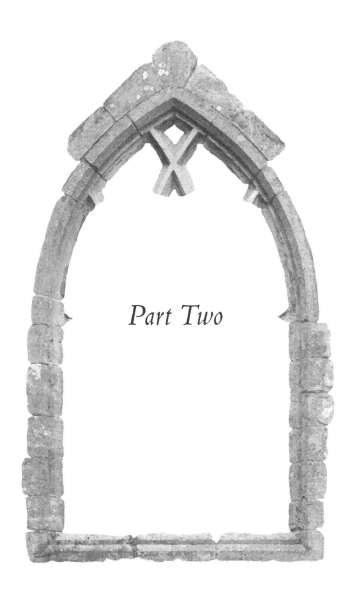

Part Two

Chapter Thirteen

1651, King's College, Aberdeen.

Kenneth Mackenzie, aged sixteen, seated in class in the midst of a lesson, is as bored as any youth of any era. The drone of the tutor's voice amid the echo and dusty smell of polished wood, lulls him into sleep. Unlike any child of any era, this Kenneth Mackenzie is the eldest son of the second Earl of Seaforth, perhaps the most powerful man in the Highlands except the King, except that for now there is no king in Edinburgh, only the English "Protector", Cromwell, and therein in lies a whole thorny problem.

Young Kenneth Mackenzie is already nicknamed "Coinneach Mór" among all the Gaelic vassals of his father's vast estates, from Kintail to Lewis, to Assynt and Strathconon. An extraordinarily tall, well-built youth whose whole mind and body have long seemed aimed towards heroism and defence by arms of the causes dear to his father and forefathers: the claim of the beleaguered fugitive King Charles the Second.

How hard to listen to the esteemed words of Master Patrick Sandylands drifting on the rarefied collegiate air, while he knows his father is in Holland with the exiled King, raising support for their overthrow of Cromwell. While the other privileged faces about him listen intently, Kenneth Mór sees them all like pampered girls for a second. He knows it is ancestral duty, as the next chieftain of Clan Mackenzie, to do something to defend the honour of his nation in the face of Cromwell's incursion.

Last year King Charles had landed at Garmouth to the great cheer of the Highlanders, only to be defeated by

Cromwell at Dunbar. The year before this, Kenneth Mór's father had moved his mother and him and his siblings, to Lewis for safety, before sailing for Holland.

This is how his mind is moving now, drifting back in time, and so it is that it eventually comes to rest on something curious, a kind of buried shipwreck lying amid the soft silt at the base of his memory.

It concerns an uncanny stranger who entered Stornoway many summers beforehand. Kenneth would have been perhaps only nine years old, their whole family enjoying the sea air that day, before these troubles started, when the country still seemed at peace…

Kenneth remembers holding his father's hand and the fine colours of his plaid. They were all on show that day before the townsfolk, as his father conferred with the town fathers, shook their hands. Crowds greeted them with genuine affection, flags were raised, ships were finely arrayed in the bay.

But again, the boy was bored. And as his mother fussed over him, he managed to lead her to the quayside, where he could see the glittering blue water, the crowds thinned out.

His mother knelt to his level. He remembers white lace and ribbons about her face, and her hand raised towards the boats in the bay, trying to get him to salute them like a little soldier. But his hand lifted and a finger pointed instead across the muddy estuary to the woods on the other side where a dark-plaided figure moved among the rocks, stopping and starting, as if engaged in an obscure dance. *Who is that fellow!?* He asked in his roundly educated vowels.

His father's hand landed on his shoulder, as he said: *What is it, Kenneth? What brings you down here?*

That man there, Kenneth said, and his father knelt too, to observe the odd stranger.

When their carriage rode around the bay and entered the castle grounds, some of his father's guards were bringing the man up from the shore to query him, but their swords were sheathed, the man was not a threat, perhaps an eccentric; they were talking to him calmly. And as the carriage drew level, the stranger lowered the cloth that had covered his head and turned his face towards them. It was as if he knew this moment and planned it: because here his astonishing face opened itself to their gaze. One eye was closed as if asleep, the skin slightly lopsided, but the skull, the forehead, the jaw were those of some Norse warrior, his good eye boring into them, a glittering diamond.

Later he remembers his feet pattering down the grand staircase to the hall, passing the suits of armour, the raised halberds, the draping pennons, oil paintings, pale faces of judgemental ancestors, the hushed scent of dark wood, as he ran towards the banqueting table to talk to his mother and father.

He remembers gazing over his father's shoulder towards the leaded glass window, the sails in the bay, and asking about the mysterious stranger. The room was like the inside of a sea chest, all dark sheen and glimmering reflections and a musty smell that drifts through his memory even now.

And what had his father said? That the stranger shared their name, he too was a Kenneth Mackenzie, but of lowly birth. That he brought a warning that English ships would come with men in metal helmets. The man was a soothsayer; he claimed to see the future in dreams. Four companies of troops would come ashore and build their own castle out of wood and earth, and subdue the Isle of Lewis. It sounded ridiculous.

Will I live to see this? Young Kenneth had asked, and his parents had laughed: *The man is a local eccentric, we should pay his stories no heed. Anyway, you will have to put on some beef if you are to fulfil his prophecy, and become a giant.*

That was all they had told him, and never spoken of it again, and yet for many hours and months thereafter as he played alone or with his siblings, his mind had secretly spun with the thrilling hope that he might magically become a giant one day.

~

Chapter Fourteen

And with this memory thus reclaimed, Kenneth Mór now stands up in class, his chair grating cruelly against the floor, and makes the weakest of excuses that he must be allowed to immediately retire to the cloakroom on account of sudden light-headedness.

As if driven suddenly by an inner light, he leaves the college by a tradesman's entrance and keeps walking, leaps over a stone wall and walks through a few courtyards until he finds a stranger's horse that suits him, and tossing a handful of guineas to the ground to cover the debt, untethers the beast, leaps into the saddle and sets off, galloping southwards, firstly through cobbled streets, then later over endless hills and valleys, jumping over dykes and streams.

It is the defining moment of his life: one of supreme freedom and exhilaration. And later, its memory will sustain him perhaps, preserve his sanity and save his soul throughout all the long six years of his subsequent imprisonment by Cromwell. In later life it will be a memory of a magnificently solitary journey south and of the huge thoughts that tumbled through his youthful head as he rode towards his destiny.

That destiny is to return from Aberdeen to Brahan then on to Kintail, raising men for the King's service everywhere he goes: the lairds of Pluscardine and Lochslinn, Tarbat, Rory of Davochmaluag, Kenneth of Coul, Hector of Fairburn.

His heart lifts as the men he meets consent to follow him, but in Kintail at last they contemplate his excessive youth and the absence of his father and conspire to humiliate him, losing the nerve for a fight without the King's orders. Before the year is out, however, they all have their chance to prove their mettle: facing Cromwell at Worcester, but to disastrous effect. King Charles himself, only recently returned, is forced to flee again to the continent.

Then the young Kenneth Mór is forced to understand the price of all his patriotism and urgent enthusiasm: fleeing Cromwell's soldiers, leaping over the dead and dying among his own men, pride only in the hope to return and fight again.

So by 1653, Kenneth Mór, his father now dead, finds himself the third Earl of Seaforth, retreated within his own estates, something of an outlaw, waiting and watching in Stornoway to see his opponent's next move, and any word of the exiled King in Flanders.

He seems almost unknown to Cromwell's men. They are not seeking his arrest, and yet when "The Fortune", one of Cromwell's small privateer ships sails into Stornoway Bay to replenish its stores, the hot-headed eighteen-year-old Kenneth Mór again seizes his chance for glory and takes the ship's officer and crew prisoners.

The privateer's captain sends a letter ashore demanding his men's release and Kenneth responds by sending his own ships out to engage them. But they are bloodily repulsed, then retreat. Now The Fortune's owner, Captain Brassie, sends word to Colonel Lilburne, officer commanding Cromwell's Commonwealth troops in Scotland, and under Cromwell's orders war ships sail from Leith under the command of Colonel Cobbet to attack Stornoway.

Kenneth Mór, Third Earl of Seaforth, has felt for a moment that his chance has come to rise to that challenge laid down somewhere in his boyhood memory: to become a giant as prophesised. But as the might of the English navy effortlessly take control of the Isle of Lewis, he finds himself a fugitive again. As he takes his last view of his pursuers from the brow of the hill above Stornoway, lamenting the loss of good men killed under his command, he sees that Cromwell's men are indeed constructing their own castle of wood and turf just as the mysterious soothsayer had described, so many years beforehand.

Seaforth's Dutch allies, wooed by his father and King Charles, seem for a while his only hope of re-taking Stornoway, until the Dutch fleet are defeated by the English off Holland, their commander Admiral Tromp killed in action. A year later, peace between England and Holland is declared, and the English look unopposed in Lewis.

Next, Cromwell sues for peace, declaring his Act of Grace and Pardon, but not for Seaforth, whose estates he seizes. By January 1655, Seaforth has been captured by Cromwell's soldiers, who burn his lands in Kintail, Loch Broom, Strathgarve, Strathconon and Strathbran as a lesson. They imprison him indefinitely in Edinburgh.

For five tedious years, Kenneth Mór stares at a prison wall. How much more hard to bear than the lesson at college in Aberdeen from which he had fled, driven by a childish dream of bravery and honour.

In 1660, Cromwell is overthrown and the Restoration suddenly saves him: King Charles II returns to power, and his loyal friend Seaforth regains his freedom, his title and his lands. He returns to Brahan Castle and almost immediately marries Isabella Mackenzie, his cousin and childhood sweetheart, daughter of Sir John Mackenzie of Tarbat, Earl of Cromartie.

There is a symmetry to their union. Her father's father had been the famous Roderick of Coigach, known as the Tutor of Kintail, uncle and mentor to the first Earl of Seaforth when he first attained power at the tender age of twelve, in recognition of which he had been granted the Tarbat title.

In 1662, Kenneth Mór is also made Sheriff of Ross, and the status of his house, his family, and his lands once again seem assured, his endurance of battle and incarceration almost vindicated.

~

Chapter Fifteen

1663, Brahan Castle, Easter Ross.

Kenneth Mackenzie sits at home at last, his trials past, relishing the long days of peace, dealing with the everyday affairs of the running of his estate, enjoying his young family, remembering the past, cherishing the future. He is now twenty-eight years old.

It is on one of these otherwise inconsequential days that Kenneth Mór's thoughts turn again to the mysterious soothsayer remembered from his childhood. His father and mother dead now, who else will remember that day in Stornoway, the untold story of who that man really was?

He stands at one of the windows of the library at Brahan Castle, the shadows of leaves playing over his face, and wonders why he is thinking about this again. Somehow it is part of his story, the reason for who he is. He feels instinctively that if that soothsayer is not known then he is not known either, and that then both their lives are equally doomed to be enigmas. The thought troubles him, this irrational craving to find that man now, and talk to him, to make sense of his own life. He had not seemed old at the time. What age would he be now? His thoughts are interrupted by a knock on the great wooden door and the entry of one of his clerks to bring him some business of the day. He pulls himself away from his reverie, his eyes coming back into focus, as he tries to engage with the everyday world again.

You will recall, my Lord, that yesterday you asked me to send for the labourer on your new bridge at Beauly who had advised his superiors that the structure will collapse. I have brought him to the castle, Sir, he waits outside.

And what is the nature of his expertise, have you ascertained that?

No, sir. He is a puzzle. He claims to be neither an engineer nor a mason, nor trained as any such. Moreover he states that he can neither read nor write.

Then how comes he by his knowledge and the authority to voice it?

The clerk looks at the floor, slightly embarrassed. *Perhaps it would be best for him to explain to you himself. He is an engaging fellow, quite harmless we are told.*

Kenneth Mór sighs, and returns to the window again, but a few moments later the sound of the next footsteps entering the room somehow wake him up, like intrusions into his soul. He spins around, and nearly faints with the resonance of the moment, the uncanny sense that his whole life is some kind of dream. *My God...* he whispers, and returns to his chair before his legs give out.

Coinneach Odhar looks down at him, arms behind his back, expression inscrutable, black hair swept back in curls, his dark plaid in shades of green and blue, that single eye scanning him, a slight twist in his lip that might be a smile, might be contempt.

My God... Kenneth Mór whispers again, then louder: *How is this possible?*

He stands up again and faces him closely, sees for the first time the detailed contours of a face that has haunted him for twenty years. They stand like reflections of each other, with the mirror taken away. *Who are you?*

Kenneth Mackenzie.

So it's true. The memories come back. That is my name also. Kenneth Mackenzie... He finds something childlike coming back into his voice as he speaks, a sense of awe moving through him.

Yes, my Lord, I know your name, of course.

But you seem unchanged, un-aged in two decades. Can that be the case? Do you remember me as a child, as I remember you?

The eye moves and looks through him, searching. *Oh yes, Sire, I have always remembered you. I saw you as you are now, even then: I saw your future. I came to warn you... but your parents' guards turned me away.*

Then you know everything. Kenneth Mór sits down again, struggling to grasp what the situation means. *You've somehow even contrived to have this meeting take place at this moment... I was about to ask my clerk to send messengers to Lewis to look for a soothsayer of your description... But you know all this?*

Coinneach Odhar nods his head.

Then what do you want from me?

Sire... Coinneach smiles unexpectedly, the reflex somehow a foreign force on his face, *I am your servant and your friend.*

Kenneth Mór gasps then begins laughing, some strange tension released in him, and goes on laughing, while Coinneach looks down at him smiling, then eventually laughing too. Finally Kenneth Mór stands up, and the two men embrace.

~

Chapter Sixteen

Drumossie Muir, April 16th 1664:
(82 years before the battle of Culloden).

From left to right: an entire horizon of peat moor, heather flickering in the breeze, a distant murmur of voices. Above it: vast sky of grey twisting clouds, occasional openings of blue, shifting shafts of sunlight. Gradually the noise builds until over the horizon a large crowd moves into view, and at their forefront a strangely solitary figure dressed in black, who moves to and fro, deep in thought as if alone on the moor, restless as a fly in a bottle.

As the crowd nears, the figure at its front stops still and the whole throng slow and gather about him, some eventually sitting down.

The man walks irregularly with a black twisted walking-stick, and one eye is blind, its iris discoloured, his face scarred and pocked. And yet the features are striking: the cheekbones pronounced, the jaw broad, the seeing eye deeply penetrating. He kneels and lifts some of the soil in his hands and holds it under his nose, breathing deeply.

For now, he closes both eyelids and meditates then turns to the crowd. He reaches into the folds of his plaid and withdraws a dark grey stone a little smaller than a child's fist and lifts it up above his head. A wave of gasps washes across the crowd and those few remaining now back away and kneel down. After a few moments he lowers the stone until it is closer to his face and places his seeing eye against the hole in its centre. He cries out:

Oh, Drumossie, thy bleak moor shall, ere many generations have passed away, be stained with the best blood of the

Highlands. Glad am I that I will not see that day, for it will be a fearful time...

His eye blinks, encircled by stone; looking upwards into the clouds. Rain falls on his shoulders, then spots of blood, then a rain of blood. Cannons fire, bodies recoil and fracture in the smoke, screams of wounded. Smoke blows across the Seer's face. When the smoke clears, hundreds of Highlanders charge headlong, broadswords raised, as volley after volley of gunshot is fired from the lines of redcoats. The bullets fire through the bodies of the Highlanders at random, tearing their breasts. The Seer recoils and shudders violently, feeling the bullets; his companions grab and restrain him, supporting him. Now he seems almost to be having a fit. Swords slice, the Redcoats slay the wounded where they are fallen, pursue women and children in the aftermath of the battle. The Seer shakes and falls to his knees. He puts his hands over his face and spits into the soil. Finally, face drained of blood, shaken to the core, he stands up and resumes his speech:

No quarter shall be given or mercy shown on either side, heads will be lopped off by the score...

His closest followers place hands on him: *Coinneach, you have never looked so ill as now. Is what you see so terrible?*

It is a terrible day, a terrible shadow that will wound our people for many generations...

Can nothing be done to prevent it, Coinneach?

The future cannot be changed, friend, though much woe may be expended to attempt it. They will know my prediction.

Recovering now, the whole entourage is moving, listening to Coinneach as he walks. *I saw the warriors, our kinsmen, our descendants. They will know this prophecy...* he repeats, *this one I have made today, before the battle takes place. They will sit by their fires in the open at night, as they flee their foes, trying to choose the place of their battle, but each of them thinking and fearing that my words will come true the next day. They will know their own doom, my friends. Yet be powerless to avoid it. They will hasten their march across this ground, hoping not to be caught here, but still they will fail and be forced to fight and fulfil the prophecy.*

Coinneach, have you no hope to give them? Look at your fellow men... you have set an icy wind among them. Their hearts are sorely burdened with this news of their future that you bring them.

Coinneach looks his friend Seòras in the eye for a long time then replies for all present to hear: *There is never any cause for despair, here or elsewhere. The future like the past, moves in waves, has peaks and valleys of both good and ill fortune. On and on, for as far as I have ever seen. I have yet to see an end of all things in the dim distances of time, and nor do I expect to. Individuals will die, as they must, but life will go on, as it must also. It is not my place to inspire, for I am no messiah. I can only report on what I am allowed to see.*

And who allows it? A voice asks from the crowd, *God or the Devil?*

Seòras draws his dagger in anger and the crowd clears: the heckler finds a hand on his throat: *The Devil resides in you, I see... or are you a simpleton? Coinneach Odhar is a prophet, not a warlock. To say otherwise might condemn him to his death by flames. Do you not understand that?*

Let him be. Coinneach intervenes. *He understands well enough.* The man flinches and shakes as Coinneach stares long and hard into his eyes. *He is afraid... one John Muir, second son of Jean.... afraid all his life I see, since his father beat him in the washhouse and took his...*

The man chokes and cries out, breaks free and runs away wailing, holding his head in his hands like a child.

Who needs a dagger when you can cut a man's mind open with words? Coinneach, what you said about what you see...

it was only half-true, was it not? We have all seen how you withhold some facts of your visions, cloak the truth in order to protect...

I protect no one. Coinneach retorts in a rasping whisper.

Not even yourself? Seòras slaps his hand on Coinneach's shoulder. *We could all understand that. When you predicted the theft of the Laird of Kilcoy's cattle, four summers ago, you were nearly hanged for the crime yourself until you saw the hiding place of the perpetrator, whose family sought you out with clubs until you mysteriously pacified them all. Since then you have grown a little more cautious with words. We have all seen the knife-edge that you walk on. Like it or nay, you are a distiller and flavourer of truth, Coinneach. Not merely its purveyor.*

Coinneach sighs and moves out slowly past the dark shoulders of his confidants as though parting curtains, and lifts his arms towards the sky and addresses the illiterate crowd, repeating and reciting his prophecy in verse for them to learn by heart.

~

Walking through the dark green hedge maze of the parterre gardens at Brahan Castle, turning left then right, Coinneach feels his destiny approaching, a shadow crossing his heart.

My children, Coinneach, and my dear wife, lady Isabella... Kenneth Mór beams as they reach the central lawn. *This is Coinneach Odhar, a seer of remarkable powers, come to assist our household and the running of my affairs...*

The black dress spins around, flowers falling from her hand, red roses. Lady Isabella, her eyes hard as obsidian. Coinneach's stomach lurches, as he remembers her as a girl, the obscure force her very existence has exerted over his life from the future, like the light of a black sun. Interrupted at their play, the children's eyes rotate and flicker inwards like rays of light, their orbits diverted, each moving, the girls to hide behind their mother's dress, the boys to precociously step forward in their little waistcoats.

Coinneach shakes their hands. *Can I have my future, please, good sir? Would you care to give up to me what is mine?*

Coinneach laughs and kneels and produces his seer stone from his pocket and lets the boys reach for it, then magically disappears it up his sleeve, then seems to find it again in his pocket. Impossible inconsistencies, one after the other, he dazzles and bewitches them.

Why can't we see it and touch it? Why won't he let us have it, Mama? The younger one pines.

The future must be won, young fellow, earned, like destiny. Coinneach answers, and hands them each a lesser trinket to amuse them, carved Pictish pebbles.

Say 'thank you' now to the stranger, my little dears... their mother reminds them, running her hands through their blonde hair, straightening the collars of their elaborate costumes.

~

Chapter Seventeen

Autumn, and snow on the ground. Coinneach returns at last to the farm of Màiri Chisholm and her father. He has long foreseen this dark shadow of bittersweet return, a reunion on a day of blinding white. He lifts the melting snow in his fingers and understands the vision at last. Màiri wears all black now, widow's weeds, as she runs to meet him across the yard from the open door, dropping her washing, recognising his stride. They embrace and weep into each other's arms. *Can it be you? After all these years...* Màiri sobs.

Coinneach sees the silver in her hair now, the crow's-feet around her eyes, but sees also that no anger or resentment resides there towards him, that she has come to understand fate now as he has, and learned to accept it.

Then like a note of hope, footsteps sound on the stone threshold and two small boys appear in the doorway of the house, shy and nervous until Màiri beckons them over. *These are James and Edward, Coinneach, my sons. Boys, this is your mother's old friend, a dear friend once to your father.*

With this, their eyes turn to each other in pain until Coinneach looks back to the boys and rubs the hair of the youngest. *Fine lads, they have the eyes of their father.* He kneels to shake hands with them, and is overcome with emotion, joy and sadness, half and half.

Her father emerges from the barn behind them, staggering a little, and Coinneach goes to greet him respectfully and sees his bloodshot eyes up close, smells the drink off him.

He feels the disturbance in his mind, his long white hair dishevelled like disordered thoughts, gets a mental flash of the fields unharvested, unharrowed and unsown. He sees the plough rusted behind him, the horses' bridles lying in the mud.

~

Màiri and Coinneach walk out together into the fields, and as Coinneach brushes against Màiri's hands and shoulders he sees the fields in flashes: through time, snow suddenly gone, different seasons, spring rain, autumn leaves, less grown or sold, slowly falling into poverty.

What befell him? Coinneach asks at last as they reach the high rise and he sees the full extent of neglect of the farm, the dykes tumbled down, fences breached, hedges outgrown into trees.

Cromwell's men... Màiri whispers, then shakes until Coinneach embraces her again and steadies herself against him. *That August they came down through Loch Broom with orders to lay waste to all of the Seaforth lands in their path. They robbed and abused all who opposed them, churches were desecrated, women dishonoured, many of the men of fighting age had not yet returned from The South. Andrew saw them coming...*

Coinneach presses his head against Màiri's cheek until he sees the pictures moving inside her mind; they move clear and sore into his heart until he pulls away, breathless with pain. The silver breast plates and helmets, men on horseback, pikes, halberds, shouting in strange accents, horses neighing. Distant church bells sounding. Torches being lifted, the season's harvest catching fire. Andrew running towards them shouting, Màiri's father trying to follow after him, still trying to get his scabbard on. A man on horseback, their leader perhaps, riding back to where the altercation is taking place and running Andrew through, left falling to his knees. The soldiers moving off, re-mounting their horses, one of them looking back, just a boy she sees now, his armour glinting, shaken by the spilt blood.

Coinneach feels the cry in Màiri's throat as it rises now in his own, and runs, then forces himself to walk to the spot where Andrew fell, half-expecting to see blood staining the snow.

We buried him at the kirkyard at Ord, Coinneach, where we three used to meet every Sunday.

Coinneach stands silently, just gazing miserably over Màiri's shoulder, to the grey veils of cloud on the horizon.

You knew, didn't you? She says drawing back suddenly. *You saw it. This was why you left? Couldn't you have forewarned us?*

And robbed you of the years of happiness you shared with him, Màiri? Robbed you of your fine sons?

Then you ran away like a coward.

No. Anger flares in Coinneach's eyes for a moment. *I set out to find the only man who could have changed this and tried to warn him…*

Who? Cromwell?

Seaforth. He was only a child back then, but I tried.

And failed?

Of course… but I found my destiny instead.

Oh Coinneach… she puts her hand on his cheek. *But you haven't aged a day, while I have grown old and grey, while my father… how can it be?*

Death and decay… let us not speak of those things any more. They turn back together towards the steadings. *They will have me soon enough, Màiri.*

~

My dear wife distrusts you, Coinneach, have you any idea why that might be so? Kenneth Mór leans back in his chair by the fire in the Great Hall, all six feet of his famous height stretching to the limits, stifling a yawn.

I warned you once, sire, you may recall. I said that there will be certain questions you may have for me from time to time whose answers I must decline to give... Coinneach cautions, where he hovers by the window, savouring the contrast of light and dark between the dark panelled walls and ceilings and the bright fields beyond, the River Conon writhing about in its shimmering blue skin, its million flickering tongues of fire; light upon the water.

Ah yes. Seaforth smiles, *Like those clan chiefs who came to visit me from Assynt and you refused to vet them as you usually do... I guessed your disquiet anyway, you know...* Seaforth looks over to check Coinneach's expression, *...and I took steps against them.*

You had them killed? Coinneach's hand tightens on the leather of the chair he passes, his eye flaring.

Now, Coinneach... we come to the questions of yours that I in turn may choose not to answer.

Coinneach's stomach rolls and pitches for a moment, as if he is back on the boat from the Long Island.

Be at peace, man. I jest. Seaforth sighs, then laughs heartily. *Then you cannot read every man's thoughts from one moment to the next, eh? I had you there!*

It is curse enough as it is, this infirmity you call a gift. Its very failings are my only respite, believe me. Coinneach reaches the fire and sits down at last. *Some people have a shadow on them...* Coinneach says after a while, looking into the flames.

Seaforth looks at him suddenly alarmed, afraid that he might be about to actually answer his question. *Lady Isabella?*

Sometimes it is some ill in their past, sometimes in their future. Malevolence. We all harbour some of that. But men get to exorcise it with their swords and bows. Sometimes powerful women lack that release until the poison festers.

I think I understand what you speak of, Coinneach. My Lady and I must live together, in mutual toleration, and so must you and she when I am called upon to go to France or Holland: have you contemplated that?

And Lowlander with Highlander, English with Scots, Catholic with Protestant... Coinneach muses. Bird song sounds from the window behind them as if in answer and he smiles.

Will a time truly come as you have said, Coinneach, when men will settle their differences with words instead of swords? I still see the faces of the men I have killed sometimes, as I fall asleep: they haunt me more, not less, as time passes. I would be glad never to bear arms again, God willing.

Assuredly such a time will come, my Lord. But the dead our descendants will walk over to reach there make a darkness almost equal to the light that leads them on.

Sounds no different from today, I fear. Seaforth stands up. *Come, Coinneach, I have much to show you. Our lands are still in ruins from The Protector's petty ravages, but I have a library full of the finest knowledge in Europe. I am eager to see how the works of those great brains will stimulate you.*

~

Seaforth rolls out a parchment map. *Here, this is the known world, the kingdoms of Scotland and England in their true shape as you have likely never seen them, and Ireland and Holland, all seen as if you are an eagle in the sky, what do you make of it?*

Here. Coinneach place his hand on the western sea. *Great cities will rise here.*

What? Atlantis? Myth and fantasy, I have Plato here in

translation about it…

No. The Americas. Where there are only outposts now. Our people will flee there from calamity.

Remarkable… Seaforth marvels, *I must show you Da Vinci and Galileo…* He suddenly looks up and changes the subject: *Is it because you are a commoner do you think? -That my Lady resents you? -That you are beneath our station? Or because you speak the Irish, and I Scots?*

Coinneach shrugs, and Seaforth becomes animated again: *But we were fated to be friends, man. Our names are the same but in different tongues, both Kenneth Mackenzie, Odhar and Mór, dark and tall, only our nicknames distinguish us.*

Perhaps it is the friendship itself, my lord, which threatens people, not our selves at all.

What madness! Would they have that we were enemies? That Seaforth should have no friends among his own people? That the poor should abhor the rich and vice versa?

Conflict and distrust are the constant order of the world, Sire, the status quo. Those who seek to make peace will never be short of enemies from each and every side.

~

Chapter Eighteen

In the dark timber study of Brahan Castle, Kenneth Mór
sets out the carved ivory chess pieces on the marble and
ebony chequerboard, and notices Coinneach lifting one of
them up and examining it strangely.

*What is it, something troubles you, Coinneach? Do you wish
me to recount the game's rules for you again?*

Not at all... Coinneach muses. *A future memory I
suppose... little carvings like these will be found centuries from
now hidden in the sand of the beach where I grew up on the
Lews. I saw them in a vision once, made by Norsemen... now
I understand their purpose.*

Scarcely has Coinneach pondered his third move, when
the door opens and a stranger is ushered in by the servants.

*Ah... my dearest brother-in-law, George, this is the local
seer I told you about, Coinneach Odhar Mackenzie, another
Mackenzie- you see we're all Mackenzies here.*

Sir George, Earl of Cromartie shakes Coinneach's hand
and eyes him closely. *Not from this parish, though, I judge
by your accent?*

From the Long Island, sire, Baile na Cille, Uig Bay...

*Oh yes, I know it well enough. A fine wild place for a lad to
grow up. How did you acquire these remarkable talents that
our chieftain has been telling me about?*

Kenneth Mór laughs. *He tells his followers some story about
a Norwegian princess for a mother, but I don't believe a word
of it. You won't get far on that avenue of enquiry, George.*

Coinneach shrugs and frowns. *It is merely a matter of
fate, sire, imponderable as a hare lip or club foot, something
common in the area or the family.*

You liken seeing into the future to a malformation, a crippled limb? Remarkable. Kenneth tells me you know the minds of his allies and enemies before he does, know what time they will arrive here before they've even saddled their horses themselves.

Coinneach and George, drawn warmly to each other, now stand either side of the leaded window, admiring the view of the elaborate parterre gardens below, the rectilinear maze of dark green hedges, the twirling parasols of Lady Seaforth and her children and maids, glimpsed as they meander to and fro in the early summer sunlight.

Careful, George... Kenneth Mór drawls, from where he sits at the chess board, *he's looking at you intently now, eyeing up your future, can you not feel it?*

George shivers involuntarily. *Pray do not tell me any bad portents.*

There are none bad to tell, sire, I see you are a man of great moral principle. You will come to hold high future office, pertaining to the law.

George and Kenneth look at each other and laugh, wide-eyed. *Well, may our one true King overhear you, Coinneach! Perhaps I should be taking you with me to France after all, to drop gossip like that around the court. Come...* Kenneth Mór stands up, *-the weather is turning too fine for this pursuit, let us descend to the gardens, shall we?*

~

Màiri's father is drunk again. Coinneach has miscalculated and arrived early, not expecting to be cornered in the house alone with him, waiting for Màiri's and the boys' return.

You are a decent man, Coinneach, albeit of a mysterious profession. They say you have the ear of Earl Seaforth, draw a salary as his advisor, yet you spend so much of your time here of late. Will you not make an honest woman of my daughter?

Your daughter is a very honest woman, sir, I know none more so. Coinneach grins.

Don't joust with me, you wily dog, or I'll thrash your back. I was wise already before you were even born. Old Chisholm looms closer, sweating.

Coinneach banishes his smile. *I have not laid a hand on your daughter sir, nor ever shall. I only seek to help you both about this place, as much as you will let me.*

Chisholm seems stunned at this for a moment. Some strange nameless antipathy rises in his eyes, animal distrust. *Is something amiss with you, man? Do you not desire of any women? They say you are an uncanny beast, though I myself have never seen anything strange about you...*

Then you have not looked closely enough. The reputation of my prophesying is spreading. A time will come soon when you might not want my name associated with this household. But my labour... and Coinneach hoists a sack of oats to his shoulder, glad to find a task to divert him from the old brute's jibes, *...my hard work and endurance are free of all names, and cost.*

The old man raises his hand in dismissive despair and makes a path to his barn again, where he thinks his stash of whisky is safe, except Coinneach has been diluting it with peaty water for weeks. Coinneach pauses at the door and looks after him and thinks that it is this barley, the kind old Chisholm drinks, that is the farm's downfall now, not the sheaves that Cromwell's horses cut down.

~

Coinneach walks on an early spring morning across the Brahan Estate. His years in the wilderness have caused his every sense to be awakened and attuned to everything around him, especially at dawn and dusk. The birdsong, the muttering of waterfalls, all of it fills him with life: sounds with more knowledge to impart than all the vanity of human words.

Passing a barn near the Loch Ussie Road, he hears a flicker of straw from within and sees Seaforth's horse tethered outside. Something inside him causes him to be cautious, and he slows his steps and maintains his way on the path to the rear of the barn, on into the woods. He pauses, then walks quietly across the grass and puts his eye to the gap between the mossy timber slats. Inside he sees the blacksmith's daughter, her skirt hitched up, and Seaforth's long black hair fallen over her shoulder, the two of them sweating, their breath clouding the morning air. Coinneach recoils from the peephole as if bitten by a snake, and returns slowly to the path, stunned, shaking, then resuming his journey hastily, filled with foreboding and appropriated guilt.

It is his day off. After lunch he takes a walk high into the hills and wrestles with his thoughts for many hours alone until he sees distant thunder cradled in the far Torridon peaks beyond Sgurr Mór.

Returning by the village of Maryburgh he chances upon a local boy playing in a meadow and gazes at his features. He has seen him before and there is something in his face, some likeness, that has always irked him. He drops by his mother's house to chat with her. She complains of Seaforth's raised taxes since the war, an unmarried woman, disgraced by the birth of her illegitimate child by an undisclosed father. He accepts her hospitality, a bowl of broth, then on parting grabs her hand on some pretext and travels for a moment backwards through her mind until he sees Kenneth Mór's face again, grimacing over her in some other barn.

What ails you?! The washerwoman asks, shivering,

disturbed by his sudden change of expression. *What have you just taken from me? Witch! Warlock!* She spits after him and crosses herself.

~

Chapter Nineteen

The Bishop of Moray calls his carriage to a halt among the streets of Inverness, and parting the red velvet of his curtains, steps down in wonder. His shoes touch the mud on the cobbles, splashing his gaiters. Hand on his wig, he turns his head from side to side to survey the crowds milling through the streets, trying to listen to the murmur and babble of whatever animates them. He calls to his footman: *What ails these souls, carriageman? I've never seen such a throng this like outside Auld Reekie.*

They have come from all around, Your Grace, from the villages and hamlets. 'Tis the Seer, they say, the Seer of Brahan is abroad on the banks of the Ness today, telling the future they say, to all that meet him.

What devilry is this? Is this man a necromancer?

No, your Grace. The footman steps backwards, a little shaken at the suggestion. *He is a pious man they say, lives but gently like a monk, and men of the cloth like yourself hold counsel with him now. His fame has spread far, this last year. He is a true seer, people say, and none that has met him doubt it.*

The bishop leans back in to talk to his scribe, and asks to borrow his cloak and hood so that he can mingle with the crowd unnoticed. Accompanied by his footman he makes his way to the river and then to the base of the hill in the castle grounds, from where he can see a black-swathed figure climbing the grass embankment, turning at the top and addressing the crowd below.

A sudden silence falls over the crowd like clouds passing over the sun, as the figure lifts a grey stone above his head. A circle of sunlight from its centre plays on his weathered face, his eyelid closed in concentration. He speaks suddenly, and many people jump a little at the sound: it is a strange voice, like a crow's caw, both jagged and melodic. The Gaelic vowels pour and twist, bright water glittering over the parched moment. The voice feels impassioned, riven by strange intensity, like a wind from another world:

I see how this town will change. I see it all clearly. People such as yourselves but in strange attire. They will be weaker and more effeminate than you, their women shameless, their ministers voiceless. But they have wondrous inventions that bring them terrible dangers. Fire and water will run under every street. Carriages without horses will run by invisible sorcery. Strings of long carriages will run on metal rails to here all the way from London, and stranger still: all the way to the Isle of Skye. Overhead, I see giant grey geese...

Somebody laughs in the crowd, until the Seer looks at them. *Don't be afraid, I am not offended, come closer.* The boy seems to be almost dragged towards the front, until the Seer reaches out and touches him and his body instantly relaxes. He turns the boy around to face the crowd, places his hand on his head then brings the stone around to cover his left eye. *Open your eyes, boy. Tell them all what you see,* he says softly. The boy blinks for a second then cries out, raising his hand to point. Half the crowd turn around also, involuntarily following his gesture: *Bridges!* He yelps. *More bridges!*

And how many do you count, boy?

His lips move, counting, his head looking about. *Nine! Coinneach, there are nine!*

And what will happen when the fifth bridge is built? What do you see there in time?

The boy blinks and then his expression changes, contorts into a sob more appropriate for a child half his age. He turns to hide his face in the folds of the Seer's cloak and is passed back into the crowd, strangers consoling him, rubbing his head. The Seer lifts his stone to his eye again, then after a moment resumes his discourse:

The present timber Bridge of Ness will be swept away while crowded with people (1675: A crowd of two hundred scream and panic, in high winds, the structure buckling, people falling into the roaring water below).

The stone Bridge that replaces it will be swept away, and on it a woman will be saved by a galloping horse (1849: Storm winds blow through Coinneach's long dishevelled hair. The pillars of the bridge each begin falling with deafening crunches from the centre out. A man runs, shouting ahead, clearing each arch just as it falls, trying to reach a woman slowed by her long white dress, he reaches her and takes her up in his arms and leaps the last yard to shore, the stone crumbling behind them into the broiling spume, clouds of dust shuddering into the air).

When the fifth bridge is built, a terrible disaster will befall the whole world (1939: Adolf Hitler barks like a vile black dog. The Seer recoils as squadrons of Stukas divebomb through the sky. He lifts his arm to protect himself. Huge grey metal armadas traverse the sea. He feels a machine gun round rattle into his body, he spits blood. Phalanxes of marching men vanish into graveyards of white crosses reaching to the horizon).

When the ninth bridge is built to cross the River Ness, fire, flood and calamity will befall Scotland (1988: The ninth bridge is completed and Pan Am Flight 103 bursts into flames in the air and falls on the town of Lockerbie. The Piper Alpha oil platform, crouching in the sea, explodes catastrophically, burning men alive. The Seer's face grimaces in the heat, his tears hissing into steam. He covers his eyes, and when he looks again the river Ness rises, flooding the town, until the rail bridge collapses).

107

The Seer's face relaxes finally, floodwaters receding across his brow. He opens his eye again and slumps, nearly fainting, his supporters catching him from either side.

Somebody shouts from the crowd: *When will this happen? How do we know it is true? Why should we believe you?*

Another man, closer to the hilltop, immediately shouts back down at him: *You dare to doubt Coinneach Odhar?*

The crowd murmurs. The Seer points at him, eye suddenly wide open again and says: *Your mother is sick, best return home, son of Donald, and take care at the Pass of the Cattle.* The man goes white and backs away into the crowd, struck with fright. Coinneach returns his attention to his audience:

All this will come to pass beyond all our lifetimes, rest assured, and none of it shall destroy this town nor its people. Life shall endure. Take heart: as Rome was, and London is, Edinburgh shall be. After many centuries and calamities, this land will return to the ownership of its people... your descendants, who will return here from distant lands as yet uncharted in the western ocean, where they will have made great fortunes.

At this a roar of approval goes up. Coinneach lifts his stone again, and then brings it down. *Scotland will lose its sovereignty in union with England...* People gasp at this and look at each other, wide-eyed.

And yet, in the future beyond that, one day, when people can walk dry-shod from England to France, Scotland shall have its own parliament once more! (In 1994 the Channel Tunnel is completed, in 1997 Scotland finally votes to restore its devolved parliament).

A great cheer goes up, and Bishop Moray pulls his cloak a little tighter around him, shivers, and gestures to his footman to accompany him, and the pair hasten away unnoticed from the back of the crowd.

~

108

Chapter Twenty

Walking towards Tomnahurich Hill, Coinneach's cousin Angus catches up with him. *What is eating at you, Coinneach? We see you are troubled.*

I do not know… not for certain at least. But I felt something black and avid watching me there, back at the castle grounds.

But the crowds were well-pleased, Coinneach, with your recital. You are a veteran now, you hold them in your power when you speak, like a statesman.

Coinneach stops and thinks. *There was something, someone among them, that I could not quite see clearly. A black hawk eyeing me as if I were a lamb. Time is growing thin here, Angus. I fear that the end I have always foreseen may soon be close at hand.*

Angus's eyes drop, his shoulders slumping. *No, do not speak in such terms, Coinneach, it will surely bring bad luck in itself.*

My future is unavoidable, as is yours. Have I not always said so?

Angus's eyes remain averted.

Well then, he slaps the younger man on the shoulder and his face lifts. *We must redouble our teaching of the verses. This is how we build a legacy. We will live in the odes and prophecies. That is where we hide, where the hawks cannot find us. They cannot touch us there.*

The crowds, strung out through the streets behind them, have begun to catch up, where they pause now at the foot of the hill. The summer rain begins to come on heavily, and everyone moves under the dense tree cover of the hill to shelter. His stone to his eye, Coinneach sees mist begin to drift through the trees.

A graveyard... He mutters, *this will become a graveyard, the town's dead buried here, but surrounded by iron railings, kept under lock and key.*

He lifts his head and looks further, beyond the trees. To his astonishment, sailing ships, rigged sails, barges, metal boats puffing steam begin to sail across the green fields beyond, travelling through what is grass on high ground, where no natural river could ever conceivably flow.

Coinneach turns around and calls out beneath the trees to those behind him: *The day will come when Tomnahurich Hill will be under lock and key, and the spirits of the dead secured within...*

People nod and mutter: *It is called the Fairy Hill,* someone whispers. *They will lock the fairies up within.*

And strange as it may seem to you this day, Coinneach continues, *a time will come, and it is not far off, when full-rigged ships will be seen sailing eastward and westward by the back of this hill* (in 1822 The Caledonian Canal is cut and completed at this point, linking together all the inland lochs of the Great Glen into one continuous waterway from west to east coasts).

As the rain ceases, Coinneach emerges onto the rise behind Tomnahurich and sees the wraith-like ships departing to the north, shifting down through stepped canal after canal, his feet on toepaths and bascule bridges yet to exist. *A marvel...* he whispers... *that men will unite to build such a wondrous thing. Ships sailing through meadows...*

Your mood is brightening now, Angus nudges him, and Coinneach turns to address the crowd: *Now remember this prediction well in verse, and teach it to your children. Here is hope and honest hard work for them to do. A great marvel will be built here. There are future blessings here beneath your feet in honest toil, just as there are curses in the shedding of blood at Drumossie.*

Is the evil one still here? Angus asks him, *Among the onlookers, the one you spoke of earlier?*

No... Coinneach sighs, his composure recovering, the trance ending as he returns to normal life, the crowd dispersing. *He left us some hours ago, I feel. Retreated, but I sense he will be back. The black eagle has marked his prey... whoever he is, he will bide his time now until he finds me lame and vulnerable, then make his strike.*

~

Chapter Twenty One

A wood pigeon plunges against the window of the vestry at Spynie Palace, startling the bishop and his scribe, Norman Matheson, in the middle of composing a sermon on witchcraft. While Norman hurries outside to investigate, he accidentally turns over a chest of drawers, dislodging various piles of old documents onto the cold stone floor. A ray of light, patterned by astragals, falls onto the old yellowed paper, and with a strange feeling of predestination, Moray finds himself kneeling down and beginning to read the handwritten missives. By the time Norman comes back inside, holding the poor bloodied bird in his hands, Moray has already decided that he has received a sign from the Almighty Himself: *Look, Norman... What astonishing providence can this be? Do you see what these are?*

Norman kneels beside him. *Commissions, Your Grace, from a century ago, signed by the hand of King James.*

Yes, yes, commissions and warrants for arrest...warrants for execution... But for what?

Poisoning, sorcery, witchcraft... it reads, under the seal.

And what names? Do you read the names, man?

William MacGillvrey, Laskie Loncart, Christine Miller...

Now further on... Down there at the bottom, see there?

Coinneach Owir... Principal enchanter.

It is a sign from God himself, Norman! A sign that we should see the wolf in our midst, that prowls and preys among our flock!

But... Norman scratches his head, grimaces. *Your Grace, this was committed to parchment one hundred years ago...*

Yes, and almost to the day and month. Do you see the date on it?

Norman nods, still troubled. *But this man cannot be the one you saw, surely, what do you mean to infer, Your Grace?*

How old can a witch grow, Norman? What shape does evil take in each generation? Can it not manifest itself in any body at will? –Bypass all and any natural laws at its twisted whim? Here is a sign, Norman. The authority of a King when it was written… but the authority of God himself now, borne by a golden ray of light and the sacrifice of a dove. Don't you see?

Norman nods solemnly, not wanting to appear slow, eager to impress in this his first year of tutelage. He jumps, as the bird he thought dead now twitches its wings on the floor where he left it by the door, and Moray goes over swiftly and takes the bird outside, leaving Norman to pore over the ancient yellowed documents himself in the cool silence. Pausing to reflect for a moment, he sees the trees of summer stirring restlessly in the breezy sunlight outside, through the high leaded windows above him.

Did it live? Norman asks on his master's return. But the Bishop turns his back and washes his hands in a bucket by the door and returns silently to put a firm hand on his charge's shoulder. *The bird? -Your Grace?*

It served its purpose. Moray says, taking the warrant from Norman's hands and pondering the small difference in a vast universe, between five and six, between w and d. *And so shall you, Norman.*

~

113

Chapter Twenty Two

From the summit of Cnoc Farrel, the Seer looks down on Strathpeffer, Dingwall. He sees the waters rising in some future time, flooding field and farms. He sets out to the valley below to warn them. But time has no sequence or order for him. Reaching the village centre, he finds metal rails buried in the bracken. He reaches down to touch them, but finds they are not in this dimension. He gasps and jumps back. A great iron engine, oily black, puffing steam like an angry dragon, narrowly misses him, hurrying to its terminus.

The Seer crosses the imaginary rails and watches the Victorian tourists of the future disembarking with their elaborate dresses and bows, men in hats and tails, their luggage carried by local lads in prim uniforms, shining their shoes. He follows them through the strangely changed streets.

At the pump house where they throw back glasses of bubbling liquid, the foul smell of sulphur rouses Coinneach to his senses. The crowd dematerialise, transforming into another one, his own people, some of them propping him up, giving him whisky to revive him, concerned for his health.

Coinneach! Should we send for a doctor? What fit is this you are having, man?

The waters of your well... foul taste and smells. He croaks.... *No, no, I don't want any of the damned stuff. But in the future, I see people with strange accents and clothes, travelling all the way from London to drink it... This town will grow wealthy, served by magical carriages without horse or bridle.*

114

He freezes, looking up at the church spire off to his left, over the shoulders of the crowd.

What do you see, Coinneach? Children are jumping up and down, the townsfolk excited by a visit from their local celebrity. *Tell us what you see!*

Ships of the sky... He marvels: *When there are five steeples in the town, strange ships will drop anchor in the sky, and moor themselves to this church spire* (Despite a petition by the townsfolk to prevent fulfilment of the prophecy, a fifth church is built, then an airship from the nearby Highland Games becomes entangled in the church spire in 1932).

The children laugh, but some of the older men seem frightened at this. *How long have we, Coinneach? You have said before that the town will flood, but we are on high ground.*

Coinneach puts his stone to his eye, and struggles, the greatest problem of all, to try to make sense and order of the fragments that he catches. *The far future... many generations...* He says at last.

The crowd sigh with relief.

Here! Coinneach goes on, *I will give you a sign to measure it by. The Eagle Stone, see there...?*

Up the hill, an ancient carved Pictish stone leans precariously in its field. *When it falls over, not once or twice, but a third time... Then will the waters have risen so far, that boats may be tethered around it.*

Coinneach approaches the stone, savouring the atmosphere around it, and kneels beside it. He presses his forehead against its cold surface, communing with the ancient forces he senses within. Seers such as himself, who have come and gone, whole aeons of unwritten history, an ancient world that is dying, coming to its end within him and in everything he does. He will be its final sacrifice, he senses, after which both he and it will pass forever beyond the reach of men, into the grey realm of unbelief and unknowing. The stone feels hard and strong, his home is ready for him, and will shelter him well.

~

Chapter Twenty Three

Lady Isabella has called Coinneach to Brahan Castle for the first time since her husband left for France. Now she turns from the window and confronts him: drinking in everything in his eye and posture. He tries not to flinch, but she has always sensed the distaste he feels for her, that he tries but rarely succeeds in hiding. She longs to ask him why he hates her.

So Kenneth Mór must be in France by now, in the court of our one true King. What are his thoughts?

Coinneach looks away for a moment at the swimming light from the lacework windows, the spring fields twisting and turning in refracted segments. *I know not.*

And he, your finest friend? And you his?

She mocks me now, Coinneach thinks, the twist of sarcasm lifting her lip like the beak of a hungry bird.

I have seen you read the thoughts of travellers, of strangers in valleys miles hence, and yet you tell me the well-being of your chieftain, your bosom brother, will not open to your fabled powers?

He shakes his head and looks down, wretched.

Then to his surprise he finds that she has come closer and runs her fingers over the muscles of his arm and chest. He looks up and she seems in a trance, her eyes far away. Then suddenly she turns around and walks away muttering: *Just get out of my sight.*

~

Arriving at the Chisholm farm, Coinneach finds Màiri in tears by the fireside, an unopened letter in her hand. Her father, sober for a change, is outside, showing the children how to work wood. He has never seen her so dejected, her eyes so dead and far away. She speaks mechanically, as if to an empty room: *My father does not know yet. He was away when Seaforth's men came by with this order. They say we are to be evicted from this land and house for being so far in arrears of our rent.*

No! Coinneach slams his fist against the wall. *Why now after so many years?* Màiri looks up, startled by his anger that she has rarely seen. *Surely there cannot be a tenant between here and Skye who is not still in arrears in the wake of the Protector's pestilence?*

Not by the amount we are, Coinneach. Let us speak plainly. My father has drunk what little revenue these lands have raised, these last ten years, and borrowed money from every fool in every tavern that has not barred him. His debts dwarf your goodwill, your labour. Andrew's death set him at war with the world and himself.

Coinneach kneels before her, miserable, as if pleading: *But in the end, this end, it is you, and the boys that he has hurt by this. Were you his intended foes in such a foolhardy war?*

Indeed not. But let us not blame him, beloved soul broken on the wheel of fate. He did not write this order. She fingers the envelope like a dead thing, the limp corpse of a white bird. *Lady Seaforth, or one of her advisors did. Do you meet with such people when you are at the castle? How can they be so cruel? You and I cannot read or write, Coinneach, but my father can. How can I let him learn of this? Oh to live in a world where our ignorance and innocence might protect us, like children.*

Coinneach laughs bitterly and they stand up and embrace. *Yes, never to read, never to know… never to read the book of God himself perhaps…*

He whispers into her ear. *What good does knowledge do*

us, Màiri? Even knowledge of the future, where does it get us in the end? Even birds and beasts are better off... Over her shoulder through the window he sees the laughter and play of the children, sunlight in their golden hair.

~

So? Lady Isabella confronts Coinneach again and he notices she wears more finery this time, jewels and bracelets and chains, as though she is growing into a Queen, nurtured on spite and distrust, drinking the murky water of reflection and echoes in her dark wooden halls.

My husband gone for a year now without a single word and still you disdain to assist me, refuse to send that uncanny mind of yours like a dove flying after him to read his thoughts and bring them home to me?

Coinneach closes his eyes, hangs his head and looks to the grain of the floorboards for strength again.

He looks up and this time she is within inches of him. He has never met a woman with breath so sour. She looks into his eyes, one alive, the other dead and sightless, like black pools, treacherous sinks in a river in spate. Her fascination is morbid, she wants to fall in but is afraid to drown.

What strange bedfellows you and I...

Please, my Lady... Coinneach winces at the impropriety of her metaphor.

She spins around, enflamed: *We are both chided, jilted, both bereaved without him, are we not? And yet what use are we to each other?*

She comes close again and looks into his eyes, catching him off-guard, and gasps: *My God... you are afraid of me, aren't you? You who fear no man, who accepts no authority, who communes with demons and angels... you fear me!*

Coinneach nods his head, too tired to pretend to disagree.

She laughs, an odd girlishness about her suddenly revealed, exultant. *I must admit some pleasure about that!*

Take care… Coinneach says, slow and considered, *…such pleasure begets pity.*

Pity?! She spits back at him. *How dare you insult me so? You think I pity myself? Or you pity me? I am as good as any man. Do you think I need Kenneth Mackenzie to run this earldom?*

I intend no insult whatsoever, my Lady. I refer to your pity for me. It will break your heart in the end, then I will be truly yours to keep forever, a bitter gift.

You speak in riddles, warlock! She mutters and turns away to the window, as Coinneach leaves the room. And she wonders how he can bewitch her like this with this shivering. The fields and trees and clouds buckle and in-bend, distorted by glass and tears, catching fire in her eyes, then dropping slowly like leaves and flags to find their cold stillness in her heart.

~

Chapter Twenty Four

Coinneach's presence within Brahan Castle has been so commonplace that he almost enjoys anonymity within the household, admitted easily through inner and outer doors by nodding staff, who hold him in less notoriety than do the crowds in Inverness now, in light of his predictions.

He passes the Seaforth children playing on the stairs, in regal costumes, hears their over-loud, educated accents. A daughter mesmerised by his gaze, two boys pretending to fire at him with cannons.

Take that scoundrel outside and horsewhip him! One of them exclaims, and a maid guarding them breaks into a grin, catches his eye, a girl from his own hamlet.

Children... She laughs. *Young Hugh is quite a tyrant today I fear, Coinneach.*

Coinneach whispers in her ear: *Children of the poor are richer in sense and manners.* She titters, blushes, a hand over her mouth, and turns away.

The wooden doors are swung open for him, and he sees Countess Isabella waits at her window seat, gazing out over the treetops, attended by a few maids who withdraw tactfully to the shadows. She writes with a quill on a leather-bound tablet.

Your ladyship. The Seer bows, and is shown to a chair.

Coinneach, good day to you, and are you in good health today?

Yes, Ma'am.

Coinneach. You will remember of course that you are to attend our celebration here this night, and that I have asked you to speak at this occasion.

Yes, of course.

Then what business have you come on this afternoon? Speak.

121

She puts down her quill, and takes up her needlework from the bench beside her.

There is a tenant farmer on Seaforth land, in the parish of Fairburn, one John Chisholm. His daughter is the widow of a late friend of mine, slain by Cromwell's rats. She told me yesterday that her father has been served with notice to be evicted from his land within the month.

The Countess sighs. *Ahhh… my husband and I have heard many such protestations from week to week over the years, Coinneach, but never before from you… you surprise me. So I am supposed to show mercy now?*

Coinneach raises an eyebrow. *With respect, I recall no evictions from Seaforth land occurring in recent memory.*

The man has been in arrears for a decade, Coinneach. Are we to have no rule of law in our lands?

He has been ill these last ten years, your ladyship, and the death of his son-in-law afflicted him sorely in mind, and the farm suffers without his labour. The widowed daughter has two young sons to raise, not yet old enough to work the land.

Why, Coinneach? Why are you asking me this now?

Perhaps if you were to delay the eviction until your husband returns from France… he tries to say but Isabella cuts him off angrily, missing a stitch and nearly pricking her thumb:

Coinneach, I am surrounded by so-called "advisors" who worry about whether my judgement is wavering in the absence of Earl Seaforth, but please do not presume to add your name to this long and tiresome list. I value your judgement in many things, your mysterious powers of reason and intuition, but politics and feudal and fiscal affairs you would do well to stay out of.

The Seer narrows his eyes for a second, then slams his hand on the desk, locking his gaze with hers momentarily, as if laying a spell. *Then I ask your forgiveness, Countess. It was not my aim to stray into the private affairs of your household, only to remind you of the general expectation of fairness among your people, and to make a plea on behalf of a disadvantaged friend.*

He rises and makes to leave, but slows as he crosses the room, until he hears the voice behind him sigh again: *Wait, Coinneach. I hope this is the last of such entreaties I can expect to receive from you?*

Now she walks across the room, leaving her needlework aside, and stands close to the Seer, face to face. *I wouldn't want to think that the basis of our relationship was beginning to change, that you thought I was vulnerable in my husband's absence.*

Coinneach breathes in and stands up straight, and shakes his head.

She continues: *This fame and esteem which gather about you of late… was it not this household that first promoted you into noble company, that set your name abroad among the genteel families of the kingdom, permitted you to travel freely without the accusation of witchcraft chasing your heels?*

Yes, Countess, for which I am truly…

But there's something else here, is there not? This girl, Chisholm's daughter, what is she to you? Then Isabella laughs suddenly in his face, before he can even answer: *Surely not?! –After all this time? –Does the great Coinneach Odhar have a heart after all? Have you fallen for something so ordinary as a woman?*

The Seer snorts, not a little annoyed. *She is merely a friend, Countess, exactly as I said, no more. And I do have a heart, and compassion for all men and women.*

And I do not?

You know such was not my insinuation.

Then let us make a bargain, Coinneach Odhar Mackenzie, a gentleman's agreement, a solemn vow, now that you're mingling with the aristocracy. I will write off this debt belonging to your "lady friend"…

Her father's debt. It is not hers, as I said.

…in return for one thing. She inches closer, and for a second Coinneach's mind drifts, he remembers her as a nine-year-old girl jumping down from a visiting carriage at Brahan Estate, playing with her regal-sounding friends, coming up to taunt him and other farm-hands. He was younger himself then, he remembers that strange gaze they exchanged then, before she was old enough to understand her status, to feel safely aloof from everything.

His eyes return to her, but she has seen him flinch for a second. Perhaps she even guesses which memory plays inside his head. *Tonight…* she exalts, *in front of all our guests, I will ask you to use your gifts to see to France, to look to where my husband is and what he is doing.*

Coinneach's gaze darkens.

And I want you to tell, tell everyone, exactly what you see, and no half-truths, Coinneach, no holding back. I know you hold back, and I will know if you do, and if I suspect so, then our bargain will be forfeit.

Coinneach's whole body begins to slump with a terrible weight of darkness, of foreboding.

Yes, Coinneach… She seems almost delighted now, in a twisted way. *We both know that something may be amiss there, do we not? Well, let us drag it out into the light of truth, this very night. That is what you will do for me. You will spy upon my husband with that unearthly eye of yours.*

She starts to turn away, but turns back again, pleased with herself, her lips pursing into something resembling a smirk. *You see, you think you can look into everyone's minds, do you not? We are all glass to Coinneach Odhar, everyone is afraid of him. But I can see into you a little, Coinneach, maybe more than a little. I have known you long enough to be sure of it. I am not afraid of you.*

For a few still seconds, time and occasion and status seem to peel away, and the Seer and Countess face each other like carved chess pieces, glassy hard and dark, their eyes meeting and reflecting, one exultant, the other grown weary with apprehension. Coinneach turns to leave.

Oh... and Coinneach... she says, driving home her advantage, *On the subject of advisors, some people have been asking strange questions about you recently.*

He lifts an eyebrow, reluctantly.

Isabella thinks better of this, and turns away. *You might meet one of them this evening.*

~

In Coinneach's small whitewashed cottage on the shore of Loch Ussie, he stands in the doorway, watching the rain drip from the thatch. Sensing that Màiri will be approaching, he returns to stoke the fire.

She enters, shaking the shawl from her hair and they sit together at the fire. The cottage is almost entirely bare apart from a few hides and furs, scarcely a bothy, since he spends so much time outdoors.

Coinneach, what ails you? You look grey as the rain, and just as cold and miserable. Sometimes I think that preaching ages you more each time you do it.

You know that I am not a preacher, Màiri.

Well, yes, she laughs, her eyes playfully aglow with the firelight, *prophecies as you would have it, they seem to hurt you.*

Yes, perhaps they do, Màiri, you may very well be right. He gazes absentmindedly into the fire. *The crowds of people... when they all look at me at once, it is as if I take all of their strength into me to see further and further. That is the greatest irony perhaps. They think me gifted, but is their own power I*

125

am harnessing. I become what they believe me to be, because they believe it. Then afterwards I feel as if... He closed his eyes, trying to find the words. *As if I am some great ruined hall, that ten thousand feet have just trudged through, wearing me down like a threshold. I only borrow their strength, but somehow the borrowing makes me weaker.*

Oh, Coinneach. She sighs and reaches her hand out and places it on his head, the first time he recalls her doing so.

He looks back into her glimmering eyes, as if waking up, touches her cheek gently, then speaks, dropping his hand away and returning his eyes to the fire: *I met with Isabella Seaforth today.*

The Countess?

Yes. I think I may be able to persuade her to cancel your father's debt entirely.

He sees her surprise, the beginnings of joy, but moves quickly to contain them: *But Màiri, there is something I want you to do that is very important. I want you to leave tomorrow with your boys and go to stay with your cousin in Applecross.*

I was considering such a journey soon at any rate, but why, Coinneach? She folds her hands on her lap, like a good girl in class.

He smiles sadly. *You must trust me and do this for me, so that in return I can safely achieve what you want.*

But I do not understand, Coinneach... are you in danger? –About to place yourself in some on my account? I could not abide that.

Coinneach reaches forward and touches Màiri's cheek, then they both lean forward until their foreheads touch. He turns the ends of her long brown hair over in his fingers and sighs. He closes his eyes, and travels into her mind, takes her mind back into his and turns it around, embracing it, cradling it, rocking it to sleep. He whispers: *You will always remember that I loved you, and that my soul is at peace, and when you remember me it will only be with happiness. When you remember me, I will live again by your side. My spirit will always travel with you and protect you and your children.*

Her body goes limp and he lays her back down carefully into her chair where she can sleep for a while. Coinneach stands and goes over again to the open door and sits on a wooden stool, gazing out at the rain falling lightly, dancing in ripples on the surface of Loch Ussie, thinking of what's on the other side: the woods and the hill and Brahan Castle beyond, the evening ahead.

~

Chapter Twenty Five

As Coinneach dismounts at the castle, darkness has fallen and an old man in faded green plaid runs out of the wood to greet him: *Coinneach, Coinneach! I have had a dream... an ill portent!*

I know, Calum, I have dreamed your dream. Coinneach sighs wearily. *I saw you dream it.*

The old man gasps, wide-eyed: *The barrel of rotten apples? The crow hanging upside-down? All of it?*

All of it. I saw you dream it. He repeats, tethering his horse.

The old man smiles in awe, a toothless grin: *Your power grows, Coinneach Odhar!*

Not for much longer, Calum. He touches his shoulder and gazes for a second into the eyes of the old man, who is left blinking, gazing off into space, as Coinneach enters the House.

~

Entering the great hall, Coinneach is introduced to several notable friends and guests of the Seaforth household, some of whom are excited by rumours they have heard of his powers: a doctor from London, a student from Edinburgh, a musician from France, the Earl of Sutherland, the Bishop of Moray. He bows to shake each hand as they all pass through the vestibule, faces lit by flickering torchlight.

Coinneach Odhar, I am honoured. Doctor Fraser Wallace. Word has reached London of your remarkable powers. I would value the opportunity to examine you medically at some point!

Màrtann MacGille Mhàrtainn... *Martin Martin. Yes, two*

names the same in English. Fascinated to meet you. Originally from Skye, now a student in Edinburgh. Is it true that you can speak four languages fluently, although you are only a farm labourer who can neither read nor write?

Bonjour Monsieur Mackenzie. Je m'appelle Michel Lambert. I would love the opportunity to set some of your rhymes to music. I met your Chieftain Earl Seaforth several years ago in Paris, he spoke very highly of you...

In Gaelic, Martin Martin cuts in: *Coinneach, there is a movement afoot among the clergy to drive our language into the sea as if it were the prattle of backward devils. I am heartened to learn that you conduct your mysterious performances entirely in the Gaelic, and that your renown is being spread by it.*

Coinneach Owir... we meet at last. You have been causing quite a stir of late in these lands. These are dangerous times to be addressing crowds unless you are quite divested of religious or political bias. I would like to learn more about your humble birth, your lineage, your views on the Bible...

Later, seated at the broad wooden tables, served with good food and wine: the fire roars, the pennons unroll from the oak rafters above. There is time to talk, before the dancing and music.

Tell me, asks the doctor, *I am told that you have prophesied a great battle on Drumossie Moor, but that the Highlanders will lose. Do you know when this battle will be?*

Coinneach shakes his head, chewing on a leg of boar.

Then you are not afraid that if it is soon, then the Highlanders will be demoralised by the knowledge of your prophecy?

No, answers Coinneach, preparing to divulge something that he rarely shares, sensing that the man does not take him seriously anyway. *The future cannot be altered, Doctor. Not on any account.*

Well then, Coinneach, the doctor nods, feeling he is

making progress, –*Then why make prophecies at all?*

Coinneach smiles sadly, seeing that the man thinks he has trapped him. *Some people will take them as warnings and will act accordingly, but that changed behaviour is already part of the future, it is incorporated.*

But, but… the doctor stutters, *you might be responsible for weakening a Royalist or Covenanting cause, as the case may be, even of endangering your nation's borders by undermining morale.*

No, because I know little of politics, and what little I learn of it, I take considerable pleasure in forgetting very quickly. Causes come and go. It is the lives of ordinary people that affect me, where the most pain resides.

But why? Isn't politics everything? –Politics and history?

Those are just words. If you saw into the future you might come to understand that.

How so?

Because it is a landscape of endless hills, and it makes you long for the sea.

Martin Martin intervenes: *Coinneach, I have a question, why have you not learned to read and write?*

My culture is one of word of mouth, sir.

The oral tradition, quite so.

When we pass on information, we must look each other in the eye. When words are written, on the other hand, we cannot be sure of the writer's true intent, nor the truth of what he writes.

But does time not blur memories? Do facts not become unreliable over time, without writing?

Not to me.

But all men do not have your abilities!

Are you quite certain of that? Perhaps they do, but they are simply unaware of the fact, or unable to accept it.

The doctor cuts in again: *What is it like to see the future, where in your mind does the vision appear to you?*

It is like a daydream or a memory, except of course that it comes from somewhere deeper. It plays across my eye, my mind's eye. I can still see what is happening in front of me, but at the same time another train of events starts moving in my head, transparently. But it quickly dominates, through some emotional grip that catches me. I become unanchored, sea-sick, adrift in the ocean of time. It is quite a distinct feeling, and usually a frightening one, but practice and familiarity ease the panic of it. The visions have their own state of motion, like somebody else's memories. They are alien, unfamiliar.

How do you know that some of these visions are not memories?

I would recognise my own past, but as to whether a vision is from the future or the past then you are quite right. Both occur. This is why I try to learn the history of each area that I visit, from the local people… it helps me make sense of what I see. And generally speaking, the less sense it makes, the more likely it is to come from the future.

Can you see a remote present?

Sometimes. But it is easier with a blood relation, or an acquaintance. Of course, people are often of the same clan, and more or less related, hereabouts.

Can you make a prediction at any time, for instance for me now, of what might happen tomorrow?

Coinneach sighs and closes his eyes, and for a moment the guests think they have insulted him, until he looks up again and mutters an incantation:

In a crooked spire
Rings a broken bell
An old crow sings
The song of a cuckoo.
Smoke, lies, cries
The fire defies.

Minstrels enter the hall, and strike up music from a gallery under the eaves, to the delight of the guests, and the fascination of Michel Lambert. The Bishop of Moray tugs on Coinneach's sleeve: *Mackenzie, when you see into the future, as you look through that darkness, do you ever see the afterlife, the souls of the dead in heaven... or in hell?*

I do not, Your Grace.

Then do you still believe there is an afterlife?

Of course, Your Grace, this is what Christ has shown us and what his church continues to impart through the scriptures. I believe it completely.

But your prophecies seem to suggest that the future is predestined, that Man's free will can have no part to play in it.

I am no philosopher, nor a minister, Your Grace, but in Gaelic we have an ancient word for this idea: freasdal, or providence. This means that the future is predestined, and although we are judged for all our actions, nonetheless the future will not be changed in consequence except by God's will.

Gaelic you say, and ancient words. And how ancient are you, Coinneach Owir?

Your Grace?

You have attained some fame of late, and I wondered how long it had taken you to accumulate. What age are you now?

I forget, exactly, Your Grace... not elderly yet.

Coinneach, I have a question for you. If I told you I had heard once of a man in my parish who was at least a hundred and fifty years old and in good health, what would you say to that?

Coinneach shrugs, perplexed by the question. *God's earth contains many wonders. But I would want to meet such a man in person, to have some evidence from his neighbours, before I could believe such a thing completely.*

Quite so, Coinneach, quite so...

Eventually, Countess Seaforth rises from her table and

claps her hands, and the minstrels depart:

Dear honoured guests and clansmen, this night as many before it, sadly, we still await news of our chieftain Earl Seaforth, Kenneth Mór, the much loved guardian of these lands. As yet, no word of him has returned from Paris, and in the absence of any further possible course of action, I have asked our renowned local soothsayer Coinneach Odhar to dine with us and thence to delve into the dark ether for us and see what fragments of truth he may bring to light. Coinneach is a long and dear acquaintance of the chieftain, and he has often told me that a crowd or gathering enhances his powers of divination, as if perhaps the gift can harness the dormant abilities of others in his deft hands. Let us pray that is so, in this instance. Please, Coinneach...

Coinneach stands up slowly, pushing his chair back, and an awed silence falls over the hall. He brings the stone out from his plaid lightly, almost playing with the thing like a trinket, grimaces at it, then lifts it to his eye:

Fear not for your lord. He is safe and sound, well and hearty, merry and happy...

Something of a sigh of relief, scarcely audible, spreads across the room, like a wave washing towards Lady Seaforth. *But Coinneach, what more do you see of him? How is he presently engaged? Why does he delay so his return, and neglect to write to us?*

The Seer keeps his stone down in his hand and says quietly, eyes fixed on the floor: *Please, Countess, ask no more of me. Just accept in good faith the truth of what I have seen, that he is well, and that good sense dictates that he will choose to return home in due course.*

No, Coinneach. Anger rises in her voice, and the guests seem to draw in their breath a little. *You must tell us all that you see, for we can all surmise that you are trying to conceal something now. This is a matter of grave importance after all, not just to me as his spouse, but to many of the other people gathered here this evening, for whom the Earl of Seaforth is their vital link to the mind of the new King Charles, protector and promoter of their interests in these uncertain times.*

Very well, Ma'am. If it is your wish then I will reveal all that I see, but all here have witnessed that I have warned you that it may not please you.

Coinneach, have you not agreed already with me that you will tell everything to me that I ask? Or have you grown forgetful of late, too immersed perhaps in more mundane matters, romancing your lady friend, perhaps?

At this some of the guests laugh, and Coinneach bares his teeth in anger. *Nay, it is not I who romances, Ma'am, nor I who forgets, nor I who abuses long-established trust.*

Breaths are taken in again, and Lady Isabella begins to look afraid as well as angry, reaching her hand down to clasp that of her sister seated beside her. *Why, what is it you mean by that, Coinneach? Is this the truth slipping from your lips now? Speak freely. Let us know the cause of this anger that animates you so, and cease to cheat us with your half-truths and riddles.*

Very well. He lifts his stone to his eye, and meditates for half a minute. *He does not talk to the King now. His business with the court is largely done. What detains him in Paris is merely pleasure rather than affairs of state. I see him on his knees, in the arms of a fair young woman of noble birth. They laugh and coo like doves in her beautiful chamber of golden tapestries and finest silks.*

Stop this at once! –A voice rings out from across the hall, but most guests are now too stunned for such composure.

In his mind he forgets Brahan Castle the while, because this young woman gives him a simple happiness which his stern and bitter wife has denied him from their very wedding night...

Some women can be heard crying now, and a few voices

are muttering, a swell of anger gathering across the hall. Isabella's face is in her hands, her sister consoling her.

Coinneach turns and walks the length of the hall, while Lady Isabella collapses back into her chair, fanned by maids and physicians.

As he looks at each of the faces at the tables, all seem to be disconsolate or mortified with embarrassment, apart from the Bishop of Moray, who sports a tender little smile as he unrolls two parchment documents from his robes and lays them out over his bench to pore over.

You insult this house! –A voice cries out from another table he passes. As Coinneach approaches the main door, the guards quiver uncertainly, as though waiting for orders. He fixes each one in turn with his stare, and they freeze, even recoiling, as he throws open the doors.

He bounds down the stairs then out into the darkness of the Castle grounds, breathing deep and clear again, eyes lifted upwards to greet the stars like melancholy friends.

~

Chapter Twenty Six

Returning to Loch Ussie through the darkened woods, Coinneach thinks he hears the spell breaking behind him, as the household begins to pull itself together. He looks up at the sailing moon which guides him, and whispers: *not long now, not long...*

He unsaddles his horse and sets it free on the moor, and climbs past his cottage, on up the slope towards the ancient fort, the wild rocky outcrop of Cnoc Farrel. From here, as the moon clears the clouds, he can see the whole landscape asleep beneath him. He sits at the edge of the cliff, and clutches his divining stone, allowing himself to drift forward and back in time, dissociating himself from the limits of his own lifespan, loosening the bonds of flesh.

Eyelid closed, he moves with the Picts and the Druids, toiling to build this enormous fortress out of stone and wood, thousands of years in the past. He inhabits the vain pride of the chieftain who paced its ramparts on wild sunlit days, feels the strength in his heart, the knowledge of the allegiance of his men, as the Irish or Romans or Vikings poured into the valleys below like puny ants. The waves of fire wipe through it and his mind is cleansed, left running his hands over the smooth rock, ramparts melted in the unimaginable heat of destruction, the fort finally destroyed. Now nobody knows what once stood here, the grass and the gulls reclaim it.

Tears fill Coinneach's eyes. He sees his mother again, running breathless across the endless expanse of sand of Uig Bay, deranged by guilt and fear of God, crying out, sun blinding her eyes. Shaking, a child again, he calls out to her, with her, in his mind, separated, estranged by time and space, but still reaching out. She runs into the waves, further and further, eyes raised to the sky, calling out to God, until salt water pours into her lungs. The sea takes her. Her long black hair twists slowly in the water like seaweed. Too late, a day later, Coinneach runs on the same beach, looking for her, finding only her footsteps in the sand, not yet erased by the tide. Barefoot, he puts his feet into her prints. Across time at last, he finds her. Mother. *Mamaidh*. The tears roll down his cheeks.

It is midsummer, and the sun will begin rising soon. Birds sing. Coinneach stands to salute the great spread of peaks to the west, the formidable ramparts of the harsh kingdom of his birth, then turns to bless with his mind the gentle hamlets below: Dingwall, Conon Bridge, Strathpeffer, the geography of all his dreams and memories. His heart is full.

It is over. Coinneach walks back down the slope, filled with a profound peacefulness and self-composure. Already the soldiers have ransacked his house and are putting torches to its thatch. Approaching them, a small group of his neighbours and relatives reach him first, as he takes out his stone and hurls it hard and long over their heads into Loch Ussie. The soldiers draw their swords, wondering if it is a missile, and turn towards him. Some foolish youth even tries to wade out to try to retrieve it, but is called back by his mother.

Coinneach raises his hands: *Nobody is to resist the soldiers, do you understand? I go willingly to accept my fate, and nobody is to spill blood trying to prevent it. Do you understand?*

But Coinneach! They say that you only told the truth. What is your crime?

Make way! The soldiers push through the gathering crowd and lift their chains towards him, turning and forming a cordon, shields up, urging the spectators to keep their distance.

Truth is crime enough! –He shouts back over their heads.

In time, Coinneach emerges, arms behind his back, and is hoisted onto horseback, to be led back towards the road. The head guard addresses him for a second, helmet under his arm: *Lady Seaforth commands that your divining stone also be taken from you.*

Coinneach laughs and the crowd jeers. *It is well gone now...* he smiles, *beneath the mud at the bottom of Loch Ussie. Only a fool will look for it presently. It will be found many generations hence, in the belly of a fish.*

The crowd almost cheer at this, but are unable to match Coinneach's unfathomable exultation, their hearts heavy as he is led away.

~

He is brought only briefly to the door of Brahan Castle, to stand at the foot of its steps while the Countess and a few advisors emerge from the unbolted doors to address him. He sees that Isabella's face is still full of shame and hurt and confusion, and that only by distilling this brew into black hatred can she find the strength to continue. Her eyes meet his, and the pain catches fire in both of them. He feels what she feels and he cannot resist the force of her emotion, nor the direction it inevitably takes her in:

You are to be burned this day at Chanonry Point, she says, her voice almost tripping with emotion, then gathering strength as she continues: *Coinneach Odhar Mackenzie, you have defamed a mighty chief in the midst of his vassals, you have abused my hospitality and outraged my feelings. You have sullied the good name of your Lord in the halls of his ancestors. For this, I shall inflict the most signal vengeance available to me. I condemn you to death.*

Coinneach lifts his head to the sky, and snorts: *Without*

even a trial? Then casts his eye over her advisors. The Bishop of Moray hands the Countess two parchments, and she says to Coinneach: *I have here two warrants for your arrest and execution for witchcraft. I see now that you are a demon, who has been engaged in the most vile intercourse with Satan himself, and that you must go to join him in that fire.*

No, Coinneach says, in a voice that somehow startles everyone with its strength: *I shall go to Heaven, but you never shall.* Some hands grapple for the hilts of their daggers at this, but they hear him out: *A dove and a raven shall fly and meet in the air above where my ashes still smoulder. Then both shall dive, but the dove shall reach the ashes first, and by this sign you may know that I shall rest in Heaven.*

The little group, Isabella at its centre, all shake their heads, heartsick at this further profanity, confirming their worst suspicions.

Take him away... Bishop Moray says.

Turning, Coinneach looks Isabella in the eyes a last time, saying: *This memory will be your torment for all eternity. I pity you for it...* before he is jostled away.

~

Chapter Twenty Seven

Countess Isabella's brother, Sir George, Earl of Cromartie, Viscount Mackenzie, is riding with some of his clansmen to visit Brahan Castle, and by mid-morning arrives at the Conon Woods. Laughing and talking as they go, sunlight playing through the leaves above, one of their number notices sombre expressions on some of the peasants they pass, who eye them strangely.

Good day to you, good sir and madam, is all well at the House ahead? I trust peace reigns in the parish this day?

Indeed not, sire. It is an ill day, for there is sore lamentation abroad. The prophet Coinneach Odhar has been put to death for witchcraft.

They stop in their tracks. *By all the stars in heaven, who tells you of this madness?*

The order came from your own sister's household, Sire, only this morning. It is said that the Seer grossly insulted her and the absent Earl Seaforth, before all assembled at the great hall, last night.

Scarcely have these words met the air, than Cromartie strikes his spurs and whip and he and his contingent race towards the castle.

Arriving at the courtyard, Cromartie leaps off his horse and bounds up the castle steps and almost knocks the guards down, storming into the hall, asking every servant as to the whereabouts of his sister, but finds many of them have been sent home. He finds her at last in the castle kitchens, holding a dead pheasant in her hands. *Sister, what is this madness that you have done?* he exclaims.

She looks at him blankly, but her face and demeanour are deranged, distracted.

Speak! Coinneach Odhar! They tell me on the road that you have ordered him put to death without trial!

He is a demon… She says. *He said last night that Kenneth Mór is in the arms of a French harlot… he said this in front of all our guests!*

While looking through his stone? And you commanded him to do this, to make this divination?

Yes, She says tossing the limp bird into a basin and turning towards the door.

Cromartie leaps past her and blocks the doorway: *But sister, Odhar never lied nor failed his people. If he spoke thus, then perchance it may be true, and the sin lies with the Earl, and now with you for having forced Odhar to speak of it.*

What of it? She snaps. *What of the authority and honour of this household? How are we to maintain it?*

What of it? He almost whispers. *What of it? Have you any idea what you have done? Do you not believe in God, in Christ his son? You may have murdered an innocent man for the sin of another, for your vanity, for your jealousy? You dispense justice on a whim, in one rash moment, but God will weigh your soul for all eternity…*

But the people must respect me… she stammers.

Isabella… He pleads, reaching his face and hands out towards her: *They will despise you, and so will Kenneth Mór, ere he returns. How will he forgive the murder of his dearest friend, no matter the truth of his own transgressions, how will he forgive you?*

Very well, brother! She raises her hands angrily, as if clearing space about her head: *go and save him if you will, the Bishop may not have lit the pyre yet…*

May not have… what? He lives yet? Why did you not speak of this at first? Where has he been taken?

Chanonry… she whispers.

Chanonry Point? He turns to run through the hall,

shouting over his shoulder: *Pray, sister... Pray for the sake of your own soul that I am not too late.*

Isabella clasps the pearls around her neck in her tensing fist and moves towards the window, the shadow of its cruciform tracery falling across her face.

~

Martin, the student from the previous night's banquet, has found himself at Fortrose, shocked and disturbed but unable to resist the spectacle of the unforeseen turn of events. Coinneach Odhar has just gone through the town in chains, on the back of a wagon. Martin listens to the chatter of the crowd, as people swell through the streets, preparing to follow on out towards the end of the peninsula, some filling the back of carts, some on horseback, some on foot.

One man's voice seems to stand out above all the others: Martin is drawn towards him, an excited old man chattering in a comically high-pitched voice. *I've seen this man before! Before, I tell you! Coinneach Owir the enchanter, the sorcerer!* Nobody seems to be listening to him, as if he has a reputation as an old fool, so when his eyes alight on Martin, he becomes even more animated, trying to impart his information: *I saw this man, once, when I was just a boy. Twelve years old, no more, in Inverness. I saw this man brought before the town authorities for witchcraft!*

How long ago was that, friend?

Why, I am ninety years old now, everyone knows that, old Angus MacCrae, the wittering crow they call me, but... but this man looked the same then! I swear it, he has not aged a day. He escaped then, they should take care or he'll escape again today!

But that's impossible, sir, what age would that make him? I spoke with him myself only last night, and he is no witch.

You spoke to him?

The old man's eyes bulge. *Did he read your future?*

No, no, but well... come to think of it...

There you are then, what did he tell you?

Martin starts to recount the rhyme: *In a crooked spire, rings a broken bell...* But finds he is drowned out by the sound of the bells from the church behind them. By the time the noise subsides, the old man has lost interest, as the bulk of the crowds begin to head for Chanonry.

Martin turns around and notices that the bells have a curiously broken sound, as if the surface of one is cracked, and examines the unusual structure of the spire: a kind of chevron-stitchwork of lead battens, some currently in the process of repair, timbers wind-damaged towards the top.

~

Chapter Twenty Eight

Gaining the high ground at the centre of the Black Isle, after several miles Earl Cromartie begins to see smoke rising from where the execution is being prepared. He spurs his horse harder and harder, until its sides bleed and the mare shrieks, nostrils flaring. He takes shortcuts over fields to speed his way. Praying to God, to take his side and slow time down, to make him something more than human for a moment, to save his sister, his family, from the stain of this black sin that now climbs the sky and sea before him, a smudge on all eternity.

~

At Chanonry Point, the Seer is brought forward to face the Bishop of Moray by the soldiers, and the gathering crowd call to him, held back by a temporary cordon of ropes and soldiers with pikes. The pyre has been constructed along with a scaffold to receive the tar barrel at its centre. The barrel itself is to one side, and the oil tar within it has now been heated beneath a separate fire: the surface bubbles, approaching boiling.

Before raising his voice, Bishop Moray brings his face close to Coinneach Odhar's, and narrowing his eyes, stares intently at him then whispers: *Who are you? What are you?* Then before he can answer, he steps back, still facing Coinneach, and shouts aloud: *Coinneach Odhar Mackenzie, do you repent? Do you confess your allegiance to the Devil? It may not be too late to embrace Christ, if you but bare your soul to God's truth...*

Coinneach clears his throat and answers, hoarse, but just

as loudly: *I have nothing to repent. I have never followed the Devil. I have only striven to speak God's truth as God revealed it to me...*

And the House of Seaforth? Do you not retract your foul slander of their good name?

Let me speak on that... he says, and turns to face the crowd: *I see into the far future, and I read the doom of the family of my oppressor. The long-descended line of Seaforth will, ere many generations have passed, end in extinction and in sorrow...*

The crowd gasps and recoils, the Bishop and his assistants shake their heads, one of them begins to take notes with a quill upon a tablet.

In Coinneach's mind's eye, pictures come into focus and play like fragments of tapestries, the fruit of previous divinations. *I see a chief, the last of his house, both deaf and dumb* (He sees the face and figure of this man, the family resemblance, senses his suffocated world, the silence that surrounds him, sees him pacing the corridors of Brahan Castle, gazing tearfully upon the portraits of his ancestors).

He will be the father of four fair sons, all of whom will die childless before he does (He sees the youngest killed in a childhood accident, the last, though an esteemed soldier and scholar, dying a slow and painful death in the south of England).

He will live careworn and die mourning, knowing that the honours of his line are to be extinguished forever, and that no future chief shall bear rule at Brahan or Kintail. After lamenting over the last of his sons, he himself shall sink into the grave, and the remnant of his possessions shall be inherited by a white-hooded lassie from the East, who is to kill her own sister (Around the open grave the assembled mourners weep, the face of one of the children turns and grows into a woman in a horse-drawn carriage returning from

145

Strathpeffer with her sister, something startles the horse, the carriage overturns. Blood spatters across her garment, a white hooded cloak, the sister's skull fractured, a stone monument later erected at the site of the tragedy).

And as a sign of when these things will come to pass, there will be four great lairds, allies and neighbours of the family, in the days of this last deaf and dumb Seaforth: Gairloch, Chisholm, Grant, and Raasay, with these deformities; one buck-toothed, one hare-lipped, one half-witted, one a stammerer. When Seaforth sees these signs he will know that his four sons are doomed to death, his land is to be sold to strangers, his race is to come to an end...

The crowd have fallen silent, only the waves of the sea can be heard for a moment, above the bubbling of the oil and the flames beneath it.

Prepare him, says Bishop Moray, his eyes grown dark and cold. *May God Almighty have mercy on your soul, Coinneach Owir.*

The guards tighten ropes about Coinneach, remove his chains, then force him down into a kneeling position. The crowd protest, and the soldiers jostle the cordon line. They tie his legs up behind him until he is in a kind of reverse foetal position, with hands crossed behind. They then thread a long timber stake through the rope bindings and two soldiers thus hoist him up to shoulder height, like some grotesque trussed roast.

~

When Fortrose comes into sight, Earl Cromartie sees the smoke is thick and black and fears the worst. He cries out, a cold shiver passing over his whole body, sensing the enormity of what may be happening. Galloping through the town, he narrowly misses passers-by, who flee into doorways

146

and vennels, his horse's hooves skidding on cobbles. It is still another mile out to Chanonry Point, the long flat road beckoning across the fields, their golden sheaves shadowed beneath the pall of an unnatural cloud.

He pushes his horse yet further, until half way along the peninsula the animal collapses, and he leaps over it, to the astonishment of passers-by, then continues running, yelling out as he approaches Chanonry, dashing past temporary stalls and booths, the atmosphere of a perverse carnival, his boots skidding on the dirt.

~

Coinneach hangs upside down, and begins to writhe and cry out in protest as the soldiers move forward until he is dangling over the steaming barrel. The steam is scalding him, his screams become unbearable, the crowd beginning to wrestle with the cordon, until the signal is given and Coinneach is lowered swiftly into the barrel. Instantly his cries cease and a foul blue vapour of burning flesh is released. At a second signal, soldiers run forward from the four points of the compass and drive spears through iron rings around the perimeter of the barrel. Then each man is aided by a second soldier and the barrel is thus lifted by a circle of eight men and carried carefully to the centre of the unlit pyre and lowered into place, the spears tethered to the prepared gantries. As these withdraw, several other soldiers run swiftly forward and back with lit tapers and the whole pyre begins to catch fire.

The flames move rapidly from orange to red and white hot, as the barrel catches, the oil-tar spewing and feeding the pyre into an intense inferno. Tracts of flame lash upwards into the sky, bristling with crackling sparks, catching on the wind. The wall of heat hits everybody's faces. The glassy

147

eyes of the crowd stare disbelievingly. Men shake their heads, women dab their eyes. The Bishop reads from his Bible, his lips moving, shouting, but not a single word can be heard above the roaring of the fire.

~

Chapter Twenty Nine

Earl Cromartie arrives at Chanonry Point to find the crowd pulling back and the embers of the tar barrel collapsing into a black pool, the flames going out, the Seer's ashes spread to the four winds.

The Earl finds his hearing leaves him momentarily, and he watches as if in a dream, moving only slowly forward now, his breath coming back. A soldier moves, as if to leave the cordon and the crowd and rake the ashes, but someone holds him back and points upward to the sky, crying out.

The whole crowd seem to look upwards as a white and a black bird, a dove and a raven, both circle over the ashes, a hundred feet in the air. Suddenly the dove plummets, the raven follows, but the dove alights first, and a wave of weeping and exclamation sweeps through the crowd. Many of the spectators now look at the nearby clergy in an expectant, even hostile way.

Cromartie regains his composure, and sees the Bishop of Moray, and catching his eye they move together to talk: *What did I just witness there?* -Cromartie asks.

Greetings, Sire. More devilry. Odhar said a dove and a crow would fight over his ashes and the dove would win and take his soul to Heaven. Even in death, he is still fooling them.

When did he say this?

At Brahan Castle, this morning on the steps, as the Countess condemned him.

You were there?

I most certainly was, and that is not all. Here is what else he spouted before he died: I have had my scribe take careful note of it for you. The man put a curse upon your sister's house. The actions of a witch beyond doubt.

Cromartie looks at the scroll. *Bishop, this is a prediction, not a curse. He probably saw this years ago, and kept it from us out of kindness. I fear you have murdered an innocent man, and a well-loved friend of Earl Seaforth.*

Innocent? With respect, Sire, I must take issue with you there. And I am a greater authority than you on matters of the soul. He defamed your family and communed with the forces of darkness. I know, I was there.

Yes, I am quite sure you were there, skulking in the background. And now you have got what you wanted: one less uncanny thing that you cannot explain away from the pulpit.

Sire! You should take care not to speak like that to a man of this office! The Bishop shouts as Cromartie turns away, exclaiming after him: *He was a demon, Sire! It was unnatural what he did. This was at your sister's orders, not mine!*

*And what about this? –*Cromartie gestures with disgust to the field of ash. *Is this natural? –What you do? This barbaric entertainment? Odhar never killed a man, nor ever plotted against one, as you did against him.*

A witch is always plotting... the Bishop counters as Cromartie makes to walk away again.

He halts then turns back: *And if he had walked on water, or made the lame to walk again, would you have burnt him for that?*

You blaspheme, Sir! Such remarks do not befit your standing!

Cromartie brings his face closer again to Bishop Moray: *To take an innocent man's life is to profane, the worst profanity of all, is that not so? I have slain men in battle, but each held a sword in his hand as I dispatched him to meet his maker. You have bound and slain a lamb here today! Like a butcher. Like a coward!*

Cromartie turns and mounts a fresh horse, brought to him by a soldier. He looks back down at the Bishop from the saddle: *May God show you his gratitude for this spectacle...*

He spits bitterly, then rides off.

~

Cromartie rides back to Brahan Castle, but his whole appearance is now downcast, drained. Hours later, he dismounts, and his scabbard trails along the dirt as he loosens it and tosses it aside on the Castle steps.

Eventually, after pacing the corridors, he finds Isabella in the Castle gardens. She sits on a stone bench by a fountain, with a handful of freshly-picked flowers.

She sees him approach and says nothing. He sits down beside her, sighing. *Odhar is dead,* he says, his voice flat, without emotion. Isabella's hands stop moving, where they have been weaving and teasing the stems of the flowers.

They burned him alive, in boiling oil, in your name, in our name, in the name of the Church, the blood-soaked vengeful Church.

Do not profane… Isabella whispers, her eyes empty.

It is you who has profaned. He says, but softly, as if the anger has left him now. *Murder is a sin. Isabella, do you know what it is to kill a man? I have killed in battle, English followers of Cromwell, Scots followers of the Covenant. I have seen their faces close to mine, as my sword took the life from them.*

Do not… Isabella flinches, throwing the flowers down, as if to get up and leave.

But Cromartie places his hand on her arm, speaking softly again: *It is an easy thing to kill a man, Isabella. God does not lift his hand to stop it at the time. It is the aftermath that is terrible. And I do not mean the wounded, the butchered bodies on the battlefield that no woman's eye should ever see. Even that is easy compared to talking to their widows. I mean the empty space that a man leaves behind him. It can be like the wake of a great galleon that wrecks every small boat in the bay, even as it sails out of sight. Coinneach Odhar will leave such a wake.*

But our family's honour... Isabella says quietly, picking up the flowers again, twisting them, beginning to fray the petals, *-it must be preserved.*

Cromartie looks at her. *You were afraid that the peasants would hear of his divination about Seaforth? Well, read this...* He hands her a scroll. *This is what Coinneach Odhar told the whole crowd at Chanonry before he died. The Bishop had it written down. People will say that he has cursed us. They will all learn this by heart, just as they have learned all his other verses. We will be like all his bridges and castles that people wait to see fall, watching for the signs. And I dare say we shan't let him down.*

This is awful... Isabella gasps, reading and wiping her eyes. *He speaks of our children.*

Sister... Cromartie says, turning to her, impassioned. *If you are going to be strong and severe, then at least be just, also. Even in war there are rules and honour. Had Odhar a family? A wife? At least make reparations to someone, even if only to Christ himself.* He takes her hands and places the scroll and the broken flowers down on the bench for her, saying: *He has not even a grave...*

~

Chapter Thirty

The Countess's carriage pulls up outside the farm house of John Chisholm and she alights. The figure of Chisholm himself, unshaven, staggers from the steading, reaching for a pitchfork.

Isabella's guards step forward protectively, hands on scabbards. *How dare you show your face here?* The man growls, and the soldiers draw their swords.

Isabella places her hands on her footman's shoulder. *No, step back...* she instructs them, then louder to Chisholm himself: *I forgive you, Chisholm, hold your peace, I forgive your unwise tongue, I see you are not yourself.*

You forgive me!? –He spits.

I will not attempt to excuse my actions in your eyes, some better time perhaps. I have only come to talk with your daughter... and I mean her no harm.

Chisholm shakes his head, and another sword sheath is heard to rattle.

Please... She says, quietly at first, then louder. *Please?*

After a pause, as Chisholm stares miserably into space, she pleads: *I mean you and her no harm. I have decided to cancel your debt, but I must first convey this news in person to your daughter.*

Chisholm seems to soften a little at this and says: *She has gone west to Applecross. She stays with a cousin there, in Fearnamore.*

Thank you. She answers, then retreats into her carriage, and her men re-mount, some of them keeping their eyes on Chisholm, expressions contemptuous.

~

The Countess arrives at a thatched cottage, at the edge of a striking coastline of plummeting cliffs and white lashing waves. Warm summer evening light, late and soft, plays through the leaves of the few wind-stunted trees by the road.

After she asks directions at the cottage door, a figure inside takes her to the side of the house and points upwards to where the hill rises to the top of a sea cliff. Isabella gestures for her men to stay behind, while she begins the walk up through the long grass blowing in the wind, lifting the hem of her dress, towards where a woman in white plays with her two young sons, both blonde-haired and bare-footed.

As Isabella arrives, Màiri is stunned as she recognises her, and clumsily begins to curtsy, then gathers her sons about her, runs her fingers through their hair, then sends them to run back down the slope to the cottage to wait there with their aunt.

Your ladyship... we are honoured to see you in these parts...

You have not heard then? –Isabella gasps.

Heard what?

Isabella looks around for a second, as if grappling for words, then changes tack: *That... that...* she stammers.

Màiri's eyes widen.

That I have cancelled your debt... she blurts out.

Màiri looks at her blankly for a moment, then suddenly beaming and overcome with emotion embraces the Countess, reaching for her hand to kiss. Isabella recoils from the embrace, almost crying out, and Màiri remembers herself, suddenly hugely embarrassed, apologising profusely, starting to try to brush imaginary dust from Lady Isabella's dress.

The Countess stops her: *Please, no, no, it is fine, do not apologise, you are quite all right...*

Then a curious silence reigns for a moment, between

gusts of wind on the hilltop as the two women look at each other, one baffled, the other torn with uncertainty.

Finally seeing that Isabella's eyes have glazed over, Màiri finds the courage to ask: *But your Ladyship... why have you come here?*

Oh... oh... Isabella suddenly seems to waken up, *-I was just passing by and I heard in the village that a woman from Fairburn was here, and when they said your name... I...m-made the c-connection...*

Màiri nods her head silently, uncertainly, smiling warmly.

And there's something else, She begins, wavering, gripped with tension, *about Coinneach Odhar...*

How is he?

Isabella looks quickly at her feet then continues, *Were you planning... I mean, are you planning to marry, you and he, I mean?*

Màiri's eyes widen, and Isabella dares to look up for a second, then returns her gaze to her feet again, as she continues talking mechanically, as if addressing her shoes, a strange repressed emotion rising in her voice: *-Because I could have arranged that... I could make funds available...*

Oh your ladyship... Màiri begins, almost reaching out again to touch Isabella. *You are very kind, but I fear that you have gained the wrong idea about Coinneach Odhar.*

Isabella looks up, blinking.

He and I are only friends.

Isabella seems startled, until Màiri continues: *He is not like other men, not in that way. He is chaste, like a priest. I would gladly have married him before I met my late husband, and I would gladly marry him now, but he will never agree to such a thing. His devotion and commitment are to his people and their future. He says he has looked into his own future and seen that there is no wife there for him, no private contentment, only his work, his prophecies. Better, he says, than a lover, is a true friend who guards over your good name and your happiness... But wait!*

Màiri raises her hand in surprise, as the Countess backs away, turning around, lifting her dress and breaking into a run as she stumbles back down the slope, a hand gesturing behind her, as if warding off any attempt at pursuit. Choking back tears, her face contorting, she throws herself into her carriage and orders it to depart immediately.

Màiri is left staring after her in puzzlement.

~

Later, a mile or so along the road, the footman calls the horses to a halt, and provoked by the loud wailing from inside the cab, feels compelled to open the curtains and inquire of his mistress's wellbeing. Eventually, she takes his hand and steps down unsteadily and moves a few paces from the road, to look out from the cliffs, across the sea loch towards the vast array of the jagged peaks of the Torridon Mountains, glowing in the evening light.

Oh God, oh my dear God... what have I done?

The wind blows through her long black hair.

What have I done? –She sobs again, half to herself, half to her impassive footman. Finally she turns around fully, her eyes wild, her face red and contorted with tears, half screaming to him: *What have I done!*

She turns back towards the distant peaks, while the soldiers, relaxed and uninterested, their armour glimmering in the sunset, feed hay to their patient horses, stroking their heads.

~ ~ ~

Afterword

Probably far too much has been said and written already about Coinneach Odhar. The whole thing has become a hackneyed minefield of loose talk and disinformation. But maybe that's precisely why I felt the need to weigh in there, to try to unravel a mystery, to look for clarity. We all have our obsessions, and they are usually hard to explain or get over by their very nature. Mine is no different.

My fascination with Coinneach Odhar must have began when I was about ten years old, in the back of a family car on its way to a holiday house in Dornoch or Ullapool, as it passed by the end of a road somewhere near Conon Bridge. One of my brothers (I am the youngest of four) pointed down this extraordinarily atmospheric looking road (an avenue of very old trees, which is still there) and said something like "That's the Brahan Seer's neck of the woods…" I asked who on earth that was, and as I listened to the answer I slowly began to feel that something was being told which concerned me almost personally, an eerie feeling. To this day, I don't really know why.

Added to that, we have my otherwise extremely rational father's insistence that he had seen into the future three times during World War Two. The visions (which were received in dreams) were about quite inconsequential things, but from the start they gave me a dilemma: either my father was a madman, or the rules of time and space were not quite what we are brought up to believe they are.

Now let's clear the air. Have I ever seen into the future? No. Have I ever seen ghosts? Not in the conventional sense, but I have "sensed" quite a lot that my rational mind finds hard to dismiss. Have I ever seen telepathically, i.e. through another person's eyes? Yes, and it scared the hell out of me.

It was probably only a matter of days after that first glimpse of the Brahan Seer's heartland in Strathconon, that a copy of "The Prophecies of The Brahan Seer" was purchased for me in some seaside town and my fate was sealed. This was the 1977 reprint of the 1877 classic by Alexander McKenzie, which has been the greatest single source of most of the speculation from every quarter, said and written since. The problem with that book is that it was the first attempt to record in written form what had hitherto been a set of spoken folk tales prevalent among an often illiterate people. From the moment the book was published in 1877, the previously nebulous truth of what underlay the folk tales began to coalesce and rally around the written version as if it was authoritative. But a close look at that book reveals that it is a cobbled-together collection of often-contradictory fragments.

A lot of people had dismissed the whole thing as pure myth until 1936 when a historical record was unexpectedly uncovered, which showed that a man named Coinneach Owir (sic) had been condemned in absentia for the crime of witchcraft and poisoning, in the Fortrose area. The problem was that the date of this writ, 1577, was exactly 100 years too early to fit the whole "Fall Of The House Of The Seaforth" part of the Brahan Seer story.

To date, I believe that nobody has written better on, or studied more thoroughly, the whole mystery of who the real Coinneach Odhar might have been, than Aberdeen University Professor Alex Sutherland in his excellent book "The Brahan Seer: The Making Of A Legend", which I can recommend unreservedly to anyone seriously interested in the subject. Alex and I enjoyed a brief and very amiable exchange of views by email on the topic of his book, back in 2011, as my own book was very close to completion. His is an easy book to read (for an academic treatise) but I personally feel that for all its many strengths it still has one of the key drawbacks of academic papers: the need to push one particular concluding theory.

Truth is, the more closely you look at the historical facts and clues, and Alex has looked very closely indeed, the more the Brahan Seer's identity becomes less clear, not clearer. All we end up being able to know with certainty perhaps, is that we cannot know anything with certainty. A paradox.

Alex cites many fascinating facts, such as the occurrence of similar figures to the Seer in Germany, Ireland and among Native North Americans, very much around the same time, i.e. the time of the birth of the modern world and the gradual onslaught of industrialism. He also shows how folk memory through oral culture is believed to "run out" or become unreliable to the point of uselessness at around 200 years. These essentially sceptical arguments are compelling. But Alex's suggestion that the earlier 1577 Coinneach "Owir" could have made all the prophecies does not convince me, for one. Only a later man, perhaps a farm labourer working on the Brahan Estate could have uttered the Seaforth "curse" prophecies, since the Seaforth household per se, did not even exist a hundred years earlier.

Similarly it seems to me, that there are clues to be found that this later figure could not have uttered some of the older prophecies. Referring to the Americas as "islands as yet undiscovered in the western sea" is not a 17th century perception, as trade and travel there was well underway by then. Also a wooden bridge collapse on the Ness that forms part of the traditional prophecies attributed to Odhar, would in fact have pre-dated the life of a later man, but been consistent with an earlier one. There are probably numerous other examples of this which could be cited, such as the prediction of a MacLeod massacre of the Macaulays on Lewis, which occurred in the early sixteenth century.

Certainly it may be the case, as other people have suggested also, that these two figures, and perhaps others, became fused over time through the blurring process of oral storytelling and faulty folk memory. We should also bear in mind that in a culture short of first and last names (and the Highlands still is), there is a long tradition of giving each other Gaelic nicknames, of which Odhar (dark-skinned) would have been a common one. The name Kenneth McKenzie itself could scarcely be any less unique.

Who is to say that evidence may not yet emerge of the identity of a later Odhar figure, who may conceivably have been put to death quietly and illegally for some spurious slight against the Seaforths around 1677? Among Alex Sutherland's research can be found at least two very intriguing clues which he himself chooses to discard, since they do not fit his theorem: Firstly, that a Dingwall presbytery record of 1668 shows the church urging Lady Isabella's chamberlain to make four stubborn offenders who live on her land (one of whom is named Kenneth McKenzie) "yield obedience" to the church, for some unspecified crime. Secondly, the memoir of Lady St Helier (granddaughter of the "white hooded lassie from the east") in which she states that one "Kenneth Ogh" was burned as a wizard by Lady Isabella in retribution for remote-viewing her husband's infidelity with two women in Edinburgh (not Paris). This is testimony from within the Seaforth family themselves, whose supposed written silence on the matter has often fuelled scepticism. But why should we expect an incident of such shame, indeed one caused by shame, to be shouted about by the family responsible?

The argument against the execution of the later Seer figure goes like this: that the writers Hugh Miller or Martin

Martin would have mentioned such an incident in their books of their respective times. The counter-argument goes that the Seaforths would easily have been powerful enough to suppress written records of such an incident. But perhaps the oral silence would also require that our recently deceased seer was not a well-known figure but a minor personage, whose story took decades to spread in resonance. But one thing seems clear to me at least: that some individual living in the late 17th century must have voiced the Seaforth prophecies, and that their content seems to test somewhat our safe concepts of what the human mind should be capable of, and what laws time and space are meant to obey.

Damning, it has to be said, to the Brahan Seer myth that we have today, is the fact that the raven and dove anecdote about his death is in fact borrowed from accounts of the life of Thomas The Rhymer. But just because this must be a fabrication (albeit a very beautiful one which I couldn't resist using) does not mean that there is no truth at all at the bottom of all of this. It's just that those fragmentary facts may be so difficult to reach now, as to be almost arbitrary.

The reader will perhaps have gathered by this point, with reference to all these factual or non-factual fragments, that I have woven my own particular story in order to plot a course that makes sense (for me at least) of most of the disparate jigsaw pieces that have come down to us. This does not mean my story thinks itself true or anywhere near it. My references to Scottish history are I hope, largely accurate and appropriate, but ultimately "The Brahan Seer" is intended as just another modern myth, albeit based upon an old one. A morality play, founded upon some intriguing historical remnants. There is the truth of what happens, then there is the deeper truth of what what happened meant. While perhaps I cannot get at the first one, I ask at least to be allowed a stab at the second, from a writer's understanding of human nature and the peculiar forces of Scottish history, some of which still affect us today in this personality-crisis of a stateless nation.

Historical research is a lot easier than it used to be. Extensive freely-available online histories of the Seaforth/ Mckenzie family, and of the Stornoway area, for instance, were of great use to me. Martin Martin's extraordinary studies of the entire western islands, much admired by Boswell and Johnston, are now online at the "Undiscovered Scotland" web resource. It was probably mischievous of me to place Martin Martin at Coinneach's last supper at Brahan Castle, since he left no record of any such event, nor indeed made any mention of a seer at all at Brahan (Michel Lambert likewise). His accounts of the second-sight however, should be sought out by anyone interested in the Gaelic view of the paranormal. As a piece of social history they widen the mind to breaking point: offering a window onto a Hebridean world where every second man and his dog seem to routinely look into the future and see the dead. Like a parallel universe on which one eventually feels the rising urge to shut the door just to preserve sanity.

Lastly, I ought to mention another authority on Coinneach Odhar, Elizabeth Sutherland and in particular her novel "The Seer Of Kintail". Fortunately perhaps, I only encountered and read this book after my own was about 90% complete, but it makes an interesting comparison with "The Brahan Seer", in terms of the assumptions it shares but the differing emphases it places on characters and places. I have no criticism to make here of Elizabeth's book. It is perhaps a little less serious in intent than my own, and takes different opportunities at the expense of passing others up, but is an enjoyable and interesting read. Such is not a modest achievement, and one I will be happy if this book constitutes in a few people's eyes.

It seemed to me when I started out that nobody had yet made sense of Coinneach Odhar's story, and therefore that it was down to me to try. I wrote this book because it didn't exist yet, but look abracadabra…. now it does.

Maybe you can leave me alone now, Coinneach. Oidhche mhath.

~

Acknowledgements

Catriona Lexy Campbell, Janette Currie,
Margaret Elphinstone, David Green,
Aonghas MacCoinnich, Rona MacDonald,
Margaret Macleod, Donald McKenzie,
Agnes Rennie, Donna Scott, Bill Smith,
Jacqueline Smith, Jamie Spracklen,
Graham & Jade Starmore, Alex Sutherland,
Robin Thompson, Jennifer Thomson,
Vikki Trelfer, Dan Watt, Ann Yule.

Douglas Thompson's short stories have appeared in a wide range of magazines and anthologies. He won the Grolsch/Herald Question of Style Award in 1989 and second prize in the Neil Gunn Writing Competition in 2007. His first book, *Ultrameta*, was published by Eibonvale Press in August 2009, nominated for the Edge Hill Prize, and shortlisted for the British Fantasy Society Best Newcomer Award, and since then he has published seven subsequent novels. He has been a director of The Scottish Writers' Centre since autumn 2011. The Brahan Seer is his sixth novel.

http://douglasthompson.wordpress.com

Also by Douglas Thompson:

Ultrameta
Sylvow
Apoidea
Mechagnosis
Entanglement
Volwys
The Rhymer